Doll Face

Doll Face

Dianne Stadhams

British Library Cataloguing in Publication Data
A Record of this Publication is available from the British
Library

ISBN 978-1-907335-91-4

This edition published 2020 by The Red Telephone
Manchester, England

Vive la difference… it makes us who we are!

If not me, who?
If not now, when?
Hillel the Elder 110 BCE - 10 CE

Contents

Acknowledgements

Thanks to:

Gill James and all at Bridge House Publishing for their encouragement, support and making this novel a reality.

John Tolson, Danielle and Lels Bonanno for their belief in the project, their constructive feedback and copious glasses of wine and cups of turmeric tea.

Liz and Michael Shore… inspirational… to a life well lived.

1 Tilly

I took Jane with me to meet the psycho. She is spot on about people. Two heads are better than one Jane and me reckon... even if one of us still has a bullet lodged in our brain.

I squeezed her hand, when we entered the room. She knew I had her back. It was an okay place. Didn't smell like a hospital. Not what Jane and me were expecting. The room had drawings on the walls. Looked like they'd been done by kids... with no talent... very messy... lots of bright colours. Were the artists mad, sad or bad?

Psycho smiled and showed us where to sit. I didn't smile back. I walked directly to the empty chair and sat down. It wasn't like a sofa or anything. You couldn't slob out. But it wasn't like a school chair either. More like the seats they have in the library at my school, padded. My feet touched the floor. I was wearing my new school shoes. I tugged the hem of my dress so that it covered my knees. Mummy said it "was appropriate" to go to the interview in my school uniform.

'Boring,' said Jane. She thought I should look cool and wear jeans and trainers with my biker jacket. It's got appliquéd roses on the pockets.

The collar on my white blouse was too stiff. It itched my neck. I wanted to scratch. I glanced at Jane. I felt her tremble. Not from fear of course, Jane is brave as bullets. But that's what lack of sleep does to you.

Me and Jane had checked it out on the Internet – all the symptoms. One website advised us not to appear too agitated or too detached. Another said to refrain from fidgeting or fixating on any one object in the room. I had to look up what those words meant. Turns out they're gobbledygook for looking and acting normal. Like that was a starter! All the sites agreed that any report would begin with a physical description.

'Mong porker, that's what they'll say,' I told Jane.

'Nah de nah de nah,' she said. 'Medics aren't allowed to use terms like that.'

'Morbidly obese with Mosaic Down Syndrome then?'

Jane had nodded in agreement.

'Matilda, why do you think you've come to visit me?' Psycho asked.

I felt Jane giggle although no sound came out obviously.

'It's not nice to call me Matilda.'

'I'm sorry. I thought that was your name,' Psycho replied.

'My birth certificate says I'm Matilda Henderson-Smythe. But I'm called Tilly. Everyone calls me Tilly. I only get called Matilda when I'm in trouble.'

I felt Jane poke my thigh. Score one to me. When we were practising before the visit Jane had told me not to take any nonsense.

'*Vivir con miedo es como vivir a medias,*' she said. That's Spanish for a life lived in fear is a life half lived. Jane's a whizzo on languages.

'Then I had better call you Tilly,' answered Pyscho, 'because you're definitely not in trouble with me. So Tilly, shall we start again? Why do you think you've come to visit me?'

'PTSD, post-traumatic stress disorder. You're supposed to work out if I'm bonkers,' I replied. 'Diagnostic therapy, they said.'

'Goodness, was that how this visit was described to you?'

'I'm not bonkers, you know. And it's not a visit. Jane and me were made to come. No choice. The travel insurance pays for it, right?'

12

'I see you've done your homework, Tilly. I am a psychologist and this is the first of a number of times I hope we will meet. The sessions are not about labelling you. Anyway we're all a bit bonkers, as you call it, some of the time.'

'So why do I have to come and talk to you?'

'Your parents and teachers are concerned.'

'Oh no, not the sleep stuff again!'

'I was hoping we might just talk about your holiday during these sessions.'

I winked at Jane. I saw Psycho noted this.

'Okey dokey, what do want to know?'

'How would you describe your holiday?'

I looked at Jane, crossed and uncrossed my ankles while I thought about the question. It was a dumb thing to ask. Duh – how could anyone describe the big bazoobo? I leant forward and put on my most earnest voice, 'It was the bestest ever holiday. Better than Disneyland.'

I squeezed Jane's hand. Game on.

Psycho smiled. 'Why was that Tilly?'

''Cause the cowboys had real guns and the Indians had real blood spurting out of them.'

'How did you feel when you saw all that blood?'

'It looked just like tomato sauce. You know, like when it shoots out the side of the burger and runs down your hand. Jane's still got some on her dress. See that.' I pointed to a faded stain on a frilly cuff.

'It's hard to eat hamburgers without getting in a mess,' agreed Psycho.

'Mummy says it's a sign of good breeding to be able to handle your food with decorum. But Mummy doesn't eat hamburgers... on holidays or at home.'

'Doesn't she like them?'

'Jane says it's because Mummy is an arsehole.'

'Really?'

'I told Jane she's spot on but it isn't cool to say so. Especially if Mummy's in radar range.'

Psycho asked me if she could tape our conversation. I told her I would have to consult with Jane as she is the legal brains for us both. Psycho just nodded and I whispered into Jane's right ear. She doesn't hear so well out of her left one now.

'Collateral damage,' my Dad said. That's one way of describing a gunshot wound.

Jane was okay about the tape. I guess we both felt quite chuffed. It was just like the movies except we weren't going to be tortured first. Psycho seemed pleased and put her notebook on the glass table between us. I winked at Jane and directed her eyes toward the jar of chocolates that was also sitting there.

'How do you feel about your mother Tilly?' asked Psycho, switching on the recorder.

'You going to play this back to my mum?'

'Absolutely not,' said Psycho. 'Nobody but you and I know what's on the tape.'

'And Jane,' I reminded her.

'And Jane,' Psycho agreed.

Jane nudged me so I asked, 'Then why record us?'

'It means I can sit and listen without having to make lots of notes. Later on, after you've gone home, I can go back and think about what we've discussed. It's easier for me to help you this way. Okay?'

Jane and me figured it was reasonable. We know that sometimes grown-ups have selective memories when they want to wriggle out of doing things with you. Psycho was just being normal… for a grown-up, I guess.

'Me and my Mum have what they call a dysfunctional relationship that is not conducive to healthy pre-adolescent development.'

'Really!'

'I learnt all about it, on one of those chat shows.'

'That's interesting. I didn't know those sort of programmes were popular with your age group.'

'Jane and me love them. Specially when they have the freaks and geeks together. The best one was a man who worked as a computer whizzo in a dog refuge. He got the lost dogs back to their owners by recording their barks and storing them in a data bank. Then when people rang up and described their pet, he could not only check out what the dog looked like, he could play the bark to the person. Clever hey?'

'It's novel, I agree,' said Psycho.

'Anyway,' I continued, 'this dog man used to dress up in his wife's clothes, not at work of course, and go to a house where everybody was in fancy dress. Like proper party kit – soldiers, devils, that sort of stuff. They played really mean party games. Like the man in the dress had to be tied up and then a soldier hit him with a whip. The man said he never cried. He said it made him feel frisky. True, that's what he said.

'Jane said the game's called say-doe-mass-kiss-em. Lots of grown-ups play it. Jane and me wouldn't like it though... too rough. Some of the boys at my school would be up for the whip bit. But not if they had to wear a dress. I think some of them would cry, specially that Jeremy.'

Psycho thanked me for telling her all that. She said she'd think about those games later. She said grown-ups call it sadomasochism and it's definitely not part of the school curriculum. Then she got stuck into stuff about my mum again.

'Do you understand what dysfunctional means, Tilly?'

'Duh – of course. Doesn't work properly.'

'Very good. How do you think your dysfunctional

relationship with your mother affects things at home?' she asked.

Tell me how it doesn't. Jane says that it means my mother has an issue with trust and independence. Jane calls her she-who-must-be-obeyed, SWMBO (sch-w-umbo) for short.

Psycho wanted to know why.

''Cause SWMBO has said I'm not allowed to watch chat shows, reality shows or soap operas. Basically, anything on TV that's fun,' I told her.

'Why do you think your mother does that?'

'Says it's all in my best interests. "You'll thank me one day," she says.

'But I won't you know. And if I ever have kids I'm going to get them the biggest plasma screens that you can buy at John Lewis. I'm going to hang those TVs above their cots. And I'm going to ban all educational programmes.'

'So what do you do if you can't watch television?' Psycho asked.

I looked at my shoes and scratched the back of my neck. This was not going in a good direction. Jane winked at me. I reckoned she was giving me the thumbs up... our go-girl-go sign. So I whispered, 'I'll get into trouble if I tell you.'

'Not in my office Tilly. No one gets into trouble when they're here with me. What you say in this room is always okay. I don't tell.'

I stared at the ceiling and the floor before cocking my head to one side, 'Poke your eye and hope to die?'

Psycho leaned forward and held out her hand, 'I promise Tilly. I promise. Can we shake on it? Will that do?'

I snorted and thought about the question. I held Jane's hand really tight.

'Jane and me are not sure what the right answer is if I've

got to talk about my holiday. We saw what grown-ups say is not what they do.'

'Can you give me an example, Tilly?'

'Like Yousef said one thing. And Giselle shook his hand and said, "It's a promise." But then look what happened. So not fair.'

'Mmm, that's an interesting way to look at it,' Psycho agreed. 'I'm just one adult, Tilly. I'm paid not to tell what people who sit in that chair, the one you're sitting in now, say to me when they're in that chair. It's my job and those are the rules that I agree to work by. Does that make sense?'

'Yousef said that the world had lost all sense of fair play.'

'How did you respond to that, Tilly?'

'Didn't get what he meant then. But Yousef did what he said he would do.'

'So will I. I'll do that because I said I will. And because I'm paid to.'

'Okey dokey,' I said and put out my hand. Psycho smiled. We shook. Result... a temporary peace agreement! I knew Jane was impressed at what I'd done.

'You going to ask me about Yousef now?' I asked.

'No Tilly, not now, another time. I'm more interested in you and your family and what you do when you're not allowed to watch television.'

Hmm, I could see she wasn't going to give up. So I filled her in on our boring life.

'Daddy lets me watch football with him. When Mummy's out. "It's our little secret." That's what he says.'

Psycho nodded, 'You like your dad?'

'Yeah, whatever. Jane says he's a metro sexual.'

'Oh, what's that?'

'Jane says it's something about being an all-round rent.'

'What's a rent?'

17

'It's short for parent. Daddy's a kind of new man. Jane said he's like a born again Jamie Oliver. You know that man on the TV? Wrote a book called *The Naked Chef* about smashing potatoes? We've got a copy of it at home. I told Jane that it was just too gross. How could she imagine the rents running all round the kitchen, with no clothes on, whipping cream? Ugh.'

'You have any other secrets that you keep from your mother, Tilly?'

I shook my head. I avoided looking at her. It all went silent. I didn't feel good about it but I wasn't saying anything more after I had felt Jane's nudge. I glanced at Jane. She wouldn't meet my eyes.

'Would you be comfortable telling me about Jane? It sounds like she's very important in your life,' Psycho asked.

I smiled, 'This is Jane, my best of bestest friend. We're going to be together, forever.'

'So Jane went with you on your holiday?'

'Yes, Daddy stood up for me. So I got to take Jane on holiday. "She's a little too old to be dragging that dirty doll everywhere she goes," SWMBO said. I could feel what Jane wanted to say back, so I told her to shhhh.'

'So you talk to Jane and Jane talks back?' Psycho said.

I settled back into the chair, cradling Jane close. Here we go, I thought.

'You sound like my Mum,' I said. 'She said to my Dad, "See, she's talking to it now. Whatever will people think?" Duh – that maybe I've got my friend with me.'

'What did your father say?'

'Jane's likely to keep Tilly occupied on the flight.'

'So what happened then?'

'Game over. Jane came too. She got to have her very own adventure before we started on THE HOLIDAY TO END ALL HOLIDAYS. That's what the rents call it now.'

18

2. Jane

Ma motto is ATTITUDE.
Think that you can, then you will.
Think that you can't then you won't.
End of. Me and Tilly have written a song about it. Nothing better than singing at the top of our voices. Weez got it clocked, man.

Some dodgy, old geezer from Ireland called Oscar Wilde, who wrote plays and stuff, said, 'You should never trust a lady who tells her age. If she tells you that, she'll tell you anything.' So Ah'm not divulging how long Ah've been around. Let's just say Ah've known Tilly when she was still a bump in her mummy's tummy. Our relationship is symbiotic. We live together. We play together. We sleep in the same bed. Ah often go to school with her if there's room in her bag and her mother doesn't check. We mentor each other. It's a bit like twins. We've got a special way of communicating that only me and Tilly know.

We're not real blood relations of course. Although sometimes you'd think so. Her mother can be a mean machine just like the one in the factory that spewed me out.

Tilly has always been fat. She looked like a pumpkin when she came home from the hospital. The jaundice faded. Then she looked like a lump of jelly that changed colours… from pink when she slept to puce when she strained to fill those nappies. She was a roly-poly toddler and a complete sausage roll when she started school. The grown-ups all try and control what she eats. Tilly's got them sorted. She eats salad and seeds with her Mum. With me she raids the stashes of biscuits and sweets she gets from the kids at school and in her neighbourhood. Their parents tell them to be nice to Tilly because she is what she is. She hides the

19

stuff in our secret place. Don't ask. If Ah told you where it was it wouldn't be secret anymore would it?

Tilly also gets gifts from other kids. It's protection money. Tilly is ace at making people feel guilty for the way they treat her. Nobody wants to fall out with the biggest kid in the class. Sometimes Tilly supplements the stash with incentive contributions. She'll do someone's poetry homework as a favour. Tilly's generous that way if she likes you. We always discuss who's in favour and who's not. Changing it from time to time makes good sense. Keeps everyone on their toes.

Other biographical stuff that you maybe will find interesting is that Tilly is fourteen years old (but way older in that head of hers). She's the dux of the special needs class and is a regular brain box. Her parents spent a fortune on extra speech, occupational and physical therapists. She's the UK chess champion for Down Syndrome and she loves swimming. Ah am so proud to have a truly rounded (no pun intended) and talented buddy to share my life with.

Before Tilly went to see the psychologist we did our Internet research.

'You gotta know the game honey child,' Ah told her. 'If you know what they're playing and the rules, you're off on a winning streak.'

'I won't have to run, will I?' Tilly asked.

'Nah – it's talking stuff. You'll smash it. You gotta talk enough so the psycho dosn't think you're weird. Don't talk too much or they'll get worried you've got a condition.'

'What sort of condition?'

We spent two days researching conditions.

'You gotta watch they don't say you've got a version of honesty Tourette's.'

We had a real laugh about that and tried to find some jokes about it. Tilly and me have got a file called Funnies about Freaks. The ones on Down Syndrome are pathetic, unfunny or downright brutal. Tourette's is a new entry. We haven't met anyone yet with that condition but sooner or later we will. We find the jokes about so called normal people much more of a laugh. Our best one is, 'What did one DNA strand say to the other? Does my bum look big in these genes.' Some people don't get it and they're not special needs. What does that tell you?

Ah wanted Tilly to achieve top score at her psych interview but sometimes she is just too open for her own good. Once she told a teacher that the definition of a normal child is one that doesn't act that way very often. Tilly got into trouble for that answer... no laughs at all for her... or me.

Ma first reaction to the psychologist was reserved. She was about the same age as Tilly's mother, not young, not old. She was skinny and wore dead dodo kit – brown skirt, brown tights, brown flat shoes, a cream shirt with little flowers all over it. Her hair was brown and cut in a bob.

'Safe and dull,' Ah said to Tilly, 'but watch the eyes.'

They were emerald green and bright. She looked straight at Tilly when she spoke to her. RESPECT! She wore pink lipstick. Me and Tilly thought it was a bit bright considering her skin was sooo white. But we've seen that stuff in the fashion magazines Tilly's mum gets. Maybe the psychologist was trying the too cool for school look?

It didn't work if she was.

Ah told Tilly the psychologist wouldn't raise the weight issue, at least not in the first interview. Anyway her GP's medical file would confirm that Tilly had always been well padded.

'No change there since the big event,' Ah reassured her. 'Bang goes their possible theory on comfort eating.'

We had a giggle over that one 'cause we found a good joke online about theories.

21

Father says, 'You want to know the difference between theory and reality, huh? Ok, go upstairs and ask your mother if she would sleep with a stranger for a million dollars.'

So the son goes upstairs and a few minutes later comes back down. 'Dad, Mom said No, she wouldn't sleep with a stranger, not even for a million dollars.'

Dad replies, 'Well there you go son. In theory your mother would never sleep with a stranger. In reality, we would be millionaires.'

We definitely won't be sharing that one with Tilly's rents!

The psychologist got top marks for being a good listener. Plus she keeps a jar of yum-scrum chocolates on her desk. Me and Tilly reckon she's spot on with bribing kids to talk.

Tilly's parents subscribe to the broad education model. They pay for her to go to a school that gets results. Tilly'd super achieve anywhere she went. That's just who she is, fancy teachers or not. Tilly's Mum is of the helicopter variety, always hovering and checking out what Tilly is learning and who she mixes with.

'No riff raff,' SWMBO warns. 'Contacts are the key to success.'

She knows didley squat.

Some of those kids at Tilly's school are seriously bad news. Does she know that Rachael's dad has a conviction for fraud and changed his family name by deed poll before Rachael got enrolled? Or that Martin's mother steals jewellery from the shop where she works part-time? Tilly's pretty good at sorting the shockers out. That brat Jeremy is one of her better wins.

Part of Tilly's parents' idea on extra-curricula activities is educational holidays.

'Travel broadens the mind,' Tilly's mother says.

Me and Tilly shake our heads… not a clue. You have to

break away from the norms to learn anything new. Otherwise it's the same old thing with the same old people in just a different setting. A winter half term, beach holiday with the Henderson-Smythe's is same old, same old with sand. This time it was worse. There was a dreaded kid's club in resort.

Ah told Tilly it was time to take action and get the gossip on what to do. We hit the Internet. It was all about grown-up stuff. That's when we hatched our big plan and set up our own blog. RESULT!

Tilly was scared she would be banned. NO PROBLEM!

Ah said we should use my name as cover. We even put some words from our song up on it as a strap line. WAY TO GO!

Ah'll show you some extracts so you can see for yourself. I'm planning to expand my repertoire to include poetry. Tilly told me to go for it. The blog was a good place to test it out.

 JANE DOLL: blog bits and bobs

Attitude
Think that you can, then you will
Think that you can't then you won't

 Jane Doll to visit the Garden of Eden

Looming large is half term break
Winter sun, sand and fun
Jane Doll – you lucky duck!
The hotel promises beach and cake
Oh yeah?
In my experience
Holidays suck!!!

ANYONE BEEN THERE?

Re: Holidays in the Garden of Eden
<<<By Celebrity Watch >>>

HELLO Jane Doll you'll be in OK territory.

Check out the pics – supermodel Princess Maria Vulcanza, Hollywood babe Banksia Heart, dishy banker Dario Caviz have all stayed there. Piss up with big bucks and celebrity guests at the official hotel opening. Maybe you can score yourself a tan and totty?

Re: Holidays in the Garden of Eden
<<<By Paradise Hotels >>>

Dear Jane Doll,

PARADISE IS OPEN to you.

Be reassured that our sun-soaked, wave-lapped, palm-fringed boutique hotel will delight you. Think of your perfect home away from home.

With only 100 guests at any time the Garden of Eden offers the highest standards of service in deluxe, en-suite, thatched villas. Each has its own personal maid, splash pool and private sun bathing area for those all-over tans. Relax in the best American cotton designer kimono. Sleep well between Egyptian linen sheets. Pamper yourself with complementary organic toiletries made from local coconut oil and frangipani flower essence. Indulge with the latest choice of movies, music and entertainment.

Gourmet food can be served a deux, en famille or in either of our two five-star restaurants. Try our lobster; caught fresh each day, to understand just what food for the gods is all about. Resident chef Francoise Marlande of Loire Valley fame and two Michelin stars will delight your palate with a range of delicacies to satisfy your every desire.

Your nights can be as quiet as you like with stargazing on the beach. Or if it's razzle dazzle you desire, visit our casino and nightclub in a quiet corner of the garden away from the villas.

We look forward to your visit.

From all of us at Paradise Hotels Plc:

International Boutique hotels for discerning travellers.

Re: Holidays in the Garden of Eden
<<<By Jane Doll >>>

A* for advertising.

But what about KIDS?

Re: Holidays in the Garden of Eden
<<<By Paradise Hotels >>>

Dear Jane Doll,

RELAX.

For children we offer a separate paradise –

no parents and lots of fun things for the little ones to do and see in our Tree House Club. All staff working with children have been trained to our highest standards.

We look forward to meeting you and your children.

From us all at Paradise Hotels Plc:

International Boutique hotels for discerning travellers

Re: Holidays in the Garden of Eden
<<<By Bad Apple >>>

Jane – U is the Doll, me be Tarzan? Want to see my serpent?

Re: Holidays in the Garden of Eden
<<<By Jane Doll >>>

Rude boy – I'm going to report your Bad Apple site for abuse.

Ah mean you have to have a laugh. That advertising stuff is downright untrue, insulting and *sooo* unimaginative. As for the kid's club, it sounds like a bunch of Nazis are in charge. Tilly gave me an A star for ma poetry debut. And we dug Bad Apple even if we called him a rude boy. He sounded like fun. We decided to play a hard-to-get game with him and see what happened. Round one to us!

3. Yousef

My name is Yousef. It means God will increase. It is the Arabic form of Joseph. If I tell you who I am, will you try to understand why?

I am Muslim. But I am not a terrorist. I support the democratic process. I renounce labels like Jihad, Zionism and the War on Terror. I consider these terms to be fundamentalist rhetoric of people opposed to the essentials of humanism. I respect the right of all faiths to live peacefully. I believe respect is a universal principle that links us all. The Koran, the Bible, the Tanakh, the Rigveda and the Tripitaka are but a few of many good books that preach tolerance, diversity and the brotherhood of man. The United Nations' Universal Declaration of Human Rights enshrined these principles, in law, in 1948.

Thus I reserve my right to protest against all paths that seem unjust.

Praise be to Allah that your eyes, your ears and your heart are open to my words.

My story starts and ends with my family. I was born twenty three years, ten months and six days ago. I am the eldest of five brothers and seven sisters. My father is a fisherman. So was my grandfather and great grandfather and his father's father before that. My mother's also from the coast. Her family do not fish. They sell fish. My father's family catch the fish that my mother's family sell to the villages where we live.

So our families have always been connected.

My mother met my father when they were small children. My father went in the boat to fish with his father. My mother came to the shore with her mother to buy fish from the boats. Our families are as much part of the coast as the sea and sand itself.

If you come to my village you might think we are poor. It is true we have only a little money. We don't have many things like foreigners. There is no TV. We play our games outside and not on computers. I like football.

My father is the champion *shatranji* in our community. That's Arabic for chess. Pieces are made from shells. The board is woven from banana leaves.

Our house is simple. It has four rooms. In one the boys sleep, in another the girls. My parents have a third room to themselves when there is not a baby to feed. The fourth room is where we sit as a family. It leads out to an area covered by a tin roof but with no walls. This is where my mother and sisters prepare and cook our food. Our family shares a toilet and a place to wash with our neighbours. They are also our cousins. It has always been like this. When I marry, my bride will come and live in my family compound. We will start to build our new home with one room. My sisters will go and live with their husbands at their family compounds. In every compound all generations live side by side. In our culture we do not have old people's homes or nurseries. The old guide the young. The young help the old.

That is our tradition. It works for us.

I went to live in England after my sister married a foreigner. He paid for my schooling. I did two years at a British boarding school. One thing I learnt was that chess was invented in India over 1500 years ago. When it spread to Persia the Arabs took it all over the Muslim world. That's how it got to Europe. The Moors brought it to Spain. I told my parents. They thought it was good that I learnt about different cultures.

I liked some things about living in England. Going to see Manchester United play at Old Trafford was one of the best. I can still taste the meat pie (even a halal option was on sale!) I ate in the stands, saw the good natured chanting and Mexican waves by the crowd, felt the camaraderie of the supporters and our opponents and heard the cacophony of the tills in the megastore after the match where I bought souvenirs for my brothers. It was a magical day.

Some things I did not like, especially the weather. Sunshine makes me happy. Grey skies, damp and the cold do not. They made me homesick. I didn't complain. I knew it would be for a short time only. Then I could come back and help my family.

If I think of my life as an hour, then my time away in England seems like a minute – spent in exile.

4. Tilly

Psycho wanted to talk about "the holiday to end all holidays".

'Duh… doesn't everyone?' I wanted to say.

'What can you tell me about how the holiday started?' she began.

'It was the bestest. Even the airport was great. Not like the one in England. It was big with white shiny walls, big marble columns, no grot. We didn't have to stand in queues. Our bags got off the plane real quick. The wheels on the trolleys didn't go funny. Not like they do at Waitrose. So Daddy didn't swear. But the two boys standing near us did.

' "Fuck Rick, take a lookie at that."

' "Shit Tom, we've landed in holiday heaven."

'SWMBO gave them her death-ray look. But they weren't looking at Mummy. They were staring at two girls who were pretending not to notice them. You know like you do when you really, really want to be picked for the team.'

I eased off the chair, clutching Jane, and re-enacted the scene. Psycho liked this. She smiled.

'I know that look even though I never get picked first.'

'Why is that Tilly?'

''Cause I'm the slowest runner in my class. "Tilly the tank, Tilly the tank", they call me. But not in English or drama. In class I am Boffin Box. Jane says, "Go alpha girl, go." But I get called tsunami Tilly at the pool.'

'That doesn't sound very nice.'

I shrugged. No big deal. 'Fat kids are fat kids. I tried the death ray look.'

'Did it work?'

'Not as well as bomb dives.'

Psycho smiled again. I sat back down on the chair and rested Jane in my lap. I could feel Jane's back against my stomach. Jane and me play a game where I try and get my tummy to make noises if Jane presses against it. That makes Jane laugh. Sometimes it makes me fart. Right then we played a different game. Our four eyes stared directly across at Psycho. She stared back and didn't look away or squirm like most grown-ups do when you try the dare stare on the bus.

'What happened then Tilly, at the airport?'

'Mummy gave one of her oh-dear-looks to Daddy. He was staring at the two girls, the same ones as Rick and Tom. Then they went into rent space.'

'What does that mean?'

'It's when they talk to each other but don't really say anything. You know when I grow up I'm going to get a tattoo of a dolphin on my chest too. And I'm going to wear red knickers you can see under white shorts. Those girls looked so cool. Don't you think so?'

'I'll have to think about it and let you know,' said Psycho. 'I don't usually wear shorts when I go out.'

I wondered if she wore that skirt outside work. I hoped she didn't. It was gross. I didn't want to hurt her feelings so I didn't pass on any advice. SWMBO says, If you can't say something nice, don't say anything. Mind you, my Mum doesn't follow her own advice half the time!

'Did you talk to the girls?' Psycho asked.

'No. My tummy was hurting. I didn't feel well.'

' "You will soon, dumpling. You will soon," said my dad.

' "Daddy, my tummy hurts."

' "Yes dumpling, mine does too."

'I did try. I wasn't whingeing. I really was poorly. But SWMBO wouldn't listen as she had put on THE VOICE and told me to shut it while she sorted out the holiday.'

'How did you feel about that?' Psycho asked.

31

I shook my head, 'It wasn't my fault. I couldn't help it coming out. And Mummy looked really cross with the man who whispered, really loudly, into his walky-talky, "Geezzus Christ, puke pile near column six, arrivals hall."

'The man was called Wayne. He said he was taking us to our hotel. I told the man I wanted a drink.

' "Are you going to be sick again?" he asked.

' "I don't like you," I said.

' "Yes you do dumpling," said my dad.

'Maybe my dad didn't hear me properly so I shouted, "No, I DON'T LIKE HIM, Daddy!"

'The Wayne man got all nervy and looked away after saying to my Dad, "Completely understand – must be difficult."

'My Dad said, "We like Tilly to be treated the same as everyone else."

'Rents hey, I thought they were supposed to protect you against the world. Jane says that's not how it is anymore.'

'We live in fractured times,' she says.

'Jane reckons I'm lucky to have two. That's alright for Jane 'cause she's only got one rent – me, and I let her watch porn with me, whenever.'

Oops, I realised I'd made a big mistake.

I felt Jane gasp.

I stopped talking. Jane cuddled closer to me. I stared at my shoes.

Psycho paused. I could hear her breathing. Then she said, very softly, 'I thought you said you weren't allowed to watch television?'

'SWMBO says I'm not.'

'But you do watch it with you father? When your mother isn't around?'

Snap, I was caught out. There was no point in lying. I nodded but kept my eyes lowered.

'Do you watch porn with your Dad when your mum's out?'

'Duh, gross!' I exploded. 'My Dad is not a pervert. I told you, Daddy is a metro sexual. You need to write that down in your notes.'

'My apologies Tilly, I forgot. So tell me about watching porn with Jane?'

'Poke your eye and hope to die?'

Psycho nodded. I checked with Jane. She nodded too. 'It's like this. SWMBO says learning is good. She loves that I get homework. I can use the computer anytime I want to do research. I do lots. And my mobile phone has Internet access too. You know you can find out anything about everything in cyberspace.'

'You discovered sex on the Internet?'

'It's a secret. You promised.'

'I did Tilly. Your secret stays in this room. So can you tell me how pornography helps you with your homework?'

'Indirect gratification, it's called. It's proper science terminology, you know. The other kids used to call me names that I didn't like. Jane said that there's nothing like porn and Facebook to broaden our education. I can tell you right now Jane was spot on. Those kids can ask me anything about sex and I bet I know the answer. Jeremy, he's in my class and thinks he knows it all.

'He said, "You're lying thunder thighs."'

'So I gave all the kids the name of the site when you can see grown-ups having sex with dogs.'

'Did that make you popular?'

'Not really. But it shut Jeremy up. Lots of the kids in my class have got dogs. They thought Jeremy was a perv if he wanted to know about that sort of stuff. Nobody sat near him at lunch for two whole weeks. Result!'

'How do you feel about dogs and sex, Tilly?'

'Gross. Don't like dogs. I'm never going to do sex, not with a dog or a boy.'

'I'm sure your parents will be pleased about that.'

Jane tapped my thigh. That's code for topped the test.

'Can we go back to talking about your holiday?' Psycho asked.

'You know everyone wants to talk to me about my holiday. I'm the most popular person at school.'

'I hope that means Jeremy has been nicer to you?'

'Not really but I don't care about him anymore. My class voted me too cool for school 'cause I was on television and the front page of the paper. I've got fifteen thousand friends on Facebook. Jeremy's only got twenty. Wicked, hey?'

'Do you like chocolate, Tilly?'

What kind of question was that?

'Duh, doesn't everyone?' I asked.

Psycho offered me the jar of chocolates on the table. I unscrewed the top and went to take one. Then I saw she was looking in her note book. So I took three. I unwrapped each one, folded the foil carefully and placed it in a pocket in Jane's dress. Before I ate it, I passed it under Jane's nose so she could smell it. Psycho asked me why.

'Me and Jane always share experiences, good and bad,' I told her.

'That's very kind, Tilly.'

'Have you got kids?' I asked when I had finished eating.

'No, I haven't.'

'Is that 'cause you've got polycystic ovaries?'

I could see Psycho was surprised. Jane said it's good to throw grown-ups off the scent sometimes.

'Whoever keeps control, banks the rewards,' is Jane's motto.

Jane has lots of mottos. I write them down and learn the words off by heart. You have to be prepared.

'Words are weapons,' is another one Jane passed on to me.

'No, nothing like that, Tilly. I just haven't got round to having any as yet.'

I told her if she got some, she should make sure she listened to them like she was listening to me. 'Then you'll be okey dokey,' I said, 'and chocolate is good too.'

'Thank you Tilly, I'll try to remember that advice. Shall we talk about what happened at the airport, after you were sick?'

I told her I heard my Dad say, 'Sorry, she's usually very good with strangers. It's probably the long flight and this heat. Not used to it I guess.'

' "No problem," replied the Wayne man. He pointed to where we had to go.

'Then Mummy said, "The travel agent told us the hotel has a club for young people."

'Just what Jane and me didn't want, you understand?'

'No, what do you mean?'

'Kids' club, that meant new kids. Hello, new bullies.'

'What did Wayne say?'

'He grinned and said, "Yes madam," in a way you know is just one big lie. "All our resort hotels cater for youngsters – from age three to teenagers. We pride ourselves on our family friendly policy. A home away from home on your holiday."

' "What time does it open?" asked SWMBO.

'Jane whispered that SWMBO was a dump-a-daughter mother. She was really cross so I tried again.

' "Jane doesn't like it here either," I said.

' "She will dumpling, she will," said my Dad.

' "No she won't. She told me she hates it. And she wants a drink, NOW!"

'That's when Wayne looked at the rents and said

something to them, really quiet. Jane and me couldn't hear. Then the rents walked ahead with all our bags.'

'And you stayed with Wayne?' asked Psycho.

'He bent down and looked straight into my face. Me and Jane could see he had hate-the-kid eyes. He opened his mouth. Me and Jane could see his shiny teeth. He looked like one of those great white sharks. Then he said, "Shut up Matilda Henderson-Smythe, or I'll give you something to cry about." '

'Goodness, what did you say to him?'

' "I hate you!" Then I vomited all over his dark green shirt.

'He said, "Geezz-us Christ" again, and grabbed my hand. He kind of dragged me out of the building and pushed me into a red mini-bus.

'That's when I realised I had dropped Jane. I tried to tell them. No one would listen. Not about Jane. Not about Wayne either. My teacher told us all about grown-ups like him. You know?'

'No Tilly I'm not sure I do.'

'My teacher said some grown-ups work as child-abusers. She said they get into big trouble if they are horrible to us. And we should tell a grown-up as soon as possible.'

'What did you do?'

'I started to cry but all I got was the death ray look from Mummy AND Wayne. That's when I knew Jane and me would just have to be brave. We were on our own as far as this holiday was going. Then the bus moved off. I looked back. Guess what I saw?'

'I can't imagine Tilly. Tell me what you saw.'

'I saw fucking Rick and shitty Tom playing football with my poor Jane.'

5. Jane

This is a picture that Tilly drew of Wayne. It's primitive expressionism in style, according to the Internet. Ah'm not sure Tilly wants to be a famous artist. But as Ah told you she's a great all-rounder. Nothing she doesn't achieve if she decides to go for it. Ah reckon she should keep her options open. If Leonardo Da Vinci could be a Renaissance man, then ma Tilly can end up Millennium Madonna.

You can just feel from Tilly's drawing what a mean son-of-a-bitch that Wayne was. If that face came swimming towards you in the sea you would know it was all over and that those teeth were gonna munch right through your bones. Ma friend Tilly was right to be on alert when Wayne was in sight. He hates kids. High score awarded when she up-chucked all over his shirt. Not so impressed that the puke dribbled all over me too. At least it was Tilly's puke, Ah suppose.

Ma adventure was no less salubrious. Do you like ma patois? Ah work on it so Ah've got ma own identity.

Otherwise you just end up being someone else's doll. And living dolls get a bad press. We're seen as airheads, nothing more than a bit of arm candy that some kid lugs along to keep them quiet. Not Tilly, she's got it sorted. She knows the value of real friendship.

Me and Tilly spent a long time researching doll types from Barbie to cabbage-patch to rag and everything in between. Ah was a wonk. That's jargon for production line reject. Something out of kilter. Ah think Ah was supposed to have blonde hair and blue eyes. But it was proscribed to be long straight hair and not afro curls. My eyes don't quite match – slightly different hues of blue. It was the mouth that did it. The plan for a rosebud cutie went wobbly. Tilly says my mouth gives me attitude. RESULT!

Tilly ain't the first kid Ah've lived with. But she's definitely the most fun and demonstrates the best potential for adulthood Ah've ever seen. On our research travels we came up with a list of attributes that would make me unique. Speech was critical. Most dolls have doolally voices, silly, vacuous timbres that spew out the odd frivolous sound. But a whaa or a purring giggle isn't in ma nature.

Tilly's grandmother is a Dolly Parton fan... Ah know, Ah know... but it seems one hundred million record sales worldwide can't be wrong. Tilly loves Dolly's southern drawl. Ma name, y'all, mawnin, Ah could go on and on with the list.

It makes Tilly laugh. And a happy Tilly is an awesome experience. So... y'all say ma name first thing in the mawnin, Jane Do-o-ll and the day will be good. Barbies hate me because Ah pose a threat – intelligence and beauty. Cabbage-Patches don't do independence. Rag dolls are sad and seem to sit on shelves, symbols of past days and out of vogue. Ah tell them to cheer up. Their turn might come round again. It's a sad fact. Dolls are on the way out. Kids today want something that looks like a doll but has a battery that turns it into an entertainment machine.

Not Tilly though, she's got it nailed. Tilly wants a best buddy and something to cuddle. Soul mates, that's how Tilly describes us. What a responsibility and a privilege Ah've got in that girl.

But Ah don't use my drawl on the blog. Me and Tilly figured that was too dangerous. Someone might trace us. Better to be safe we agreed. Proper Queen's English was the best disguise.

But Ah digress. Ah was going to describe ma adventure in paradise. Let's just say it started badly. Those overgrown testosterones on two legs thought it was funny to kick me around like Ah was a football. It wasn't funny... for me. It hurt... a lot.

The short one was called Tom. His tall friend was Rick. He had gel in his hair. It stuck up like a unicorn and man did it pong. He had a silver cross and a skull in his left ear. He wore a sleeveless vest. Me and Tilly thought he did that to show off his muscles.

'Gym bunny,' Ah said to Tilly.

Rick was better looking but boy did he know it. He didn't wear any jewellery, not even a watch. His jeans were tight. His t-shirt and trainers were white as white. So were his teeth, spent some money at his dentist, that's for sure. Ah caught him looking at himself on every shiny surface in that airport... vain as a cock-a-doodle on a coop roof shooting the breeze.

After Tilly was sick Ah was a waste of space. Nobody wanted to touch me. Ah stunk of vomit. That Wayne hauled Tilly off to a mini-bus. She kept calling out for me. Nobody listens to kids. Nobody cares if a kid and her best buddy get separated that's for sure.

Rick and Tom had been chatting up two girls that had been on our flight from London. When they went off in the same bus as Tilly, Rick told Tom he was going to have a slash. Ah just don't get why boys have to use words to sound mysterious. Going to the toilet, doing a wee, is perfectly clear. Slash? Come on! Tom said he'd wait with their rucksacks.

After a while a cleaner came pushing a trolley full of mops, buckets and bottles, a proper emergency kit. Would you believe he turned out to be Yousef? Ah didn't recognise him at first when he took us hostage at the hotel the next day. At the airport he wore a dish-dash on his head. It looked like a checked t-towel. Guess that's the same as Rick wearing a baseball cap back to front. Got to look like the in-crowd.

Yousef picked me up and wiped me clean. Ah thought he was kind. Boys aren't usually nice to dolls.

Tom said to the cleaner, 'Hey mate, seen my friend? Tall guy?'

Yousef didn't seem to understand. Tom asked again, slow like and used a bit of sign language. The cleaner shook his head and stuck out his hand.

'Bloody hell, wanker,' snapped Tom. 'What a cheek, you gotta be kidding, right? A tip? I've Just arrived. I don't have a bloody razoo. Don't think you can rip me off. Anyway that doll's not yours. It belongs to the fat retard. I saw her drop it. What are you people like? Stealing a toy from a kid like that?'

'You want?' said Yousef and handed me to Tom.

'Me mate's gone missing,' Tom said. He held me at arm's length.

'Mate gone where?'

'Chasing girls for sure.'

'You want girls?' asked the cleaner.

'No I want me mate. You know a guy. Eng-lish M-A-N.'

'You want man?'

Tom nodded yes.

'You English?'

'Yes, me English man. I want English man. You understand?'

The cleaner nodded and replied, 'Yes, yes understand. Englishman want. Man cost twenty pounds. Two men same time, special deal, thirty pounds. You want boys. Cost more money. You tell me what you want. I find. Also girls you want. I can get.'

'What the fuck?' Tom shouted, ('scuse ma language but those were his exact words), 'I don't want to buy any bloody men to shag. I came with my mate. We like girls.'

Tilly's mother would have gone ballistic if she had heard those swear words. Even Tilly's Dad doesn't use the f word when he bangs his head on the car door.

'You no want men or boys. You want girls. We get you girls. How many girls you want?' the cleaner continued. I was getting scared that Tom might hit the cleaner... with me.

'Listen you fucking moron. I – NO – WANT – SEX with my mate or your girls. Okay?'

'Ah, I understand now. Sorry, my English no good sometimes. No want boys. No want girls. You are like Australian men, yes? You want goats?

'Fuck off, you pervert.'

Ah couldn't wait to tell Tilly. Perverts on holiday, we were going to have to get wifi access to continue our research on goats! This holiday was starting to improve.

Rick came back and the boys put me in one of their rucksacks and dropped me off at the hotel. Ah guess that

Rick had found out where those girls were staying after all.

This is what I put on my blog.

 JANE DOLL: blog bits and bobs

Attitude
Think that you can, then you will
Think that you can't then you won't

 Jane survives Paradise Hell

The Garden of Eden hotel
Has a**holes on holiday from hell
Hoot a horn, ring a bell
Listen to what the coconuts tell

1. Jane met the holiday rep from hell. Think Jaws in tadpole trousers!

2. Jane got separated from the love of her life. Imagine the horror!

3. Jane got assaulted by yobs having a lark. Feel the pain!

Not a LOL
Know what I mean?
HOLIDAYS SUCK!

 Re: Jane survives Paradise Hell
<<<By Armchair Traveller >>>

Stay at home Jane. You'll save time, money, trouble and the environment. Travel broadens the mind – so mind travel.
Imagine where and watch your very own documentary.

Re: Jane survives Paradise Hell
<<<By Bad Apple >>>

Jane – U is still my travelling Doll. Want to see the tadpole down my trousers?

Re: Jane survives Paradise Hell
<<<By No Regrets >>>

Take photographs. Get witnesses. Report the assault to the police.
Sue the bastards!

Re: Jane survives Paradise Hell
<<<By ♀Luv U >>>

Jane – stand firm. Name and Shame.

Re: Jane survives Paradise Hell
<<<By Jane Doll >>>

Thanks for the support By ♀Luv U.
WAYNE, WAYNE, WAYNE... arsehole rep!

Later when we checked our blog Ah told Tilly we were doing just dandy. Bad Apple was still in our orbit. How exciting to have a real life admirer. Bad Apple was getting value. Two of us... just like the stuff in the supermarkets, buy one, get one free. Man, did we giggle over that.

'You're a total grade A wit,' said Tilly and gave me a high five.

She's right. Ah am.

Here's Tilly's picture of the psychologist. Ah think you can see a definite development in her work.

43

Tilly is totally brill at capturing the essence of her subjects. What did I tell you about those eyes? Tilly rates Psycho. She says she's for real. But Ah warned ma buddy.

'Be careful,' Ah said. 'Look up psycho on the Internet. It means crazy. There's only six letters between psycho and psychologist. There's not much of a gap between being a nutter and a nurturer.'

6. Yousef

British school boys of my age are not political. Well not the ones I mixed with when I boarded in that country. They found politics boring. They sneered at politicians. None of them aspired to a career in political or public service. They wanted to be footballers, play cricket for Britain and make money. It seemed to me that all their families were rich. They could afford the school fees and drive those big cars to Speech Day.

If your family has money where I come from, you too will make money. That is just the way it is. Of course lots of boys want to be footballers and play cricket. But everyone, young and old, argues about politics. We learn the details of political systems in our history, geography, personal development... well in most lessons really.

'Everything is political,' our headmaster said, 'every decision we make, every action we take is political. What you learn will shape what you do. Knowledge makes a difference.'

My headmaster in England was more into competition. Winning and achieving seemed to be the most important goal.

Nobody... in England or my country... listens to young people. It seems they want you to learn how to be a mirror image of them. You are expected to adopt their values. British kids have a lot in common with us. Nobody wants to know how we think things could be better.

'You'll learn,' those British grown-ups would say, 'when you're older... you've got no idea... change the world... nice theory... won't work... grow up first and work out what you want to be.'

Most of my friends want to be a tourist when they grow up. We see these foreigners who come to our beaches, lying in the sun, drinking Coco Cola, eating all the time.

'What a good job to have,' my friends say. 'Being a tourist is right up there with being a celebrity. Lucky ones can do both.'

I want the world to be fairer for everyone.

That's why I decided to ask thirty British foreigners to stay behind after their meet and greet gathering. Nobody would listen to what was happening. I told my gang that we needed access to world media to tell it as it is. I know the convention is to buy space and time to advertise your message. But as you Europeans like to say, 'When in Rome...'

But here is not Rome. We don't have money to pay the media.

So we must show you another way of hearing what we want to say. The thirty gathered inside the Garden of Eden Hotel were all part of our strategy on how to speak and be heard. We know. We say. You listen. You learn. Let's call it an exercise in thinking outside the box.

The foreigners are inside the box, safe, fed and watered. Yes, their movement is restricted. This is in the interests of everyone leaving the box in the same condition they entered. Which is more considerate than how many of us have been treated by you tourists. Please permit me to explain.

The land along this coast is beautiful. But sandy soil does not produce good crops or at least not too many of them. Life is tough for local people. Not unpleasant, and we love the ways we have. But still life is tough and food is scarce. When the consultants came from Europe, they promised that tourism was the route out of poverty. We too could have jobs. Our families would have opportunities. We would benefit from tourism – with new roads, schools and health services. They said there would be training and new skills.

My community was excited. Our fishermen knew their catch would help feed the promised visitors. The young saw a future that offered choice. The old hoped for less hardship. We all dreamed of wealth and what it would bring us. The elders imagined a Mercedes and a new mosque. The youth squealed names like Nike and Gameboy. The foreign buzz words were sustainability and development.

Blue sky thinking, they called it, all things are possible.

Good joke that one. It's grey sky in your European homes. Definitely blue skies here. But whether you live in or outside a box, under rain or shine, all men recognise a gun is a gun. Not the best way to make sure the world listens, I agree. But sometimes the only way is to go direct.

After all, did not your great British parliamentarian, John Pym, say in 1628, *Actions speak louder than words?*

7. Giselle

When I look back on the interviews I feel proud. I did the job I promised to do. My sources were reliable. The range of witnesses was broad. I know I captured the personal with the news unfolding. It was a professional coup to get the scoop. I made it happen.

Not everyone sees it that way of course. The hate mail that Jane Doll Blog has directed my way is totally unfair.

'Who reads Internet stuff uploaded by someone posing as a doll?' I argued with my editor.

The figures he quoted were a surprise. Seems a lot of people out there are too dumb to know the difference between the truth and fake news.

'Don't sound so defensive,' he replied, 'but watch your back. You're young. Your first big story went global. Being judged as the liar has its benefits and costs.'

'I secured live witness interviews. They were the best.'

He agreed but wanted to know why those very witnesses hadn't refuted the stuff on the blog.

I made a large cup of ginger and lemon tea, sat down at the console and chose one of the video tapes of my interviews to play back. That Tom was a natural and he made me smile. No mean feat amidst the aftermath. I cued his introduction and pushed the play button. Tom, the tanned hunk from Essex, grinned to camera and began.

'Me mate Rick and me wanted some sun, sand, surf and lots of sex. The travel agent had a deal if we left the next day. One hundred and fifty quid for the flight. Said we could pick up somewhere to crash when we landed. Not bothered me... I can sleep anywhere. Even on the beach.

'Course I hadn't heard the name of the place we

*was flying to. Me mum was well bothered. She don't
go nowhere they don't speak English.*

*' "Never know if there'll be trouble in the
jungle," she says.*

*'Shoulda listened to her I s'pose. Not that we went
to any jungle. Have to say the holiday started well if
you know what I mean?'*

The camera cut to me. I looked blank and raised an
eyebrow. That always works. Say nothing, look lost and
your interviewee fills the space. Best way to get a
confession. All the pros use the technique. That's what our
lecturer told us.

'I'm not saying it, not on the telly.'

'Oh Tom, please just say it all in your own words. As it
comes. It's really important that the viewers get the true
story. And don't worry, the editor likes to do his bit. He'll
make sure it's okay for broadcasting. Anything you want to
say, any order. Don't be shy. Don't hold back.'

'Me mum's going to be well chuffed when she sees me
on the telly.'

'So tell me why the holiday started so well.'

*'Rick spotted two babes on the flight. Well buffed.
One was blonde. The friend was dark. Knew they
were up for a good time. The blonde had one of them
styles that looked like she'd stuck a pineapple on top
of her head. Not a real blonde. Okay I s'pose except
that you could see black roots. "Needed doing, slack
cow," me mum would say. Not my type but she gave
Rick the wink. He was well pleased. Soon as we
landed, we got our backpacks, and went to hang
round in the arrivals hall. Well chuffed we was, no
rubbish or nothing. Cleaner than Heathrow even.*

Didn't expect that in a place me mum called the dark arse of empire.

' "Hey darlin', you got a light?" Rick said to the blonde one.

' "The sign says no smoking in the terminal," replied the dark-haired one.

' "You always play by the rules?" Rick grinned.

' "Depends on the game don'it?" said the blonde.

' "You're not wrong darlin'," said Rick. "What's yer name?"

' "Sharon, call me Shazza. Me mate's called Tracey."

' "Shazza and Trace, hey? Could be your lucky day Shaz. I'm Rick. He's Tom. Where you two hanging out?"

' "Garden of Eden Hotel," said Shazza. "We got a deal on one of them self-catering suites."

' "You do breakfast?" asked Rick.

' "Depends... on what I get for dinner."

' "Cheeky, like it!" '

'Love the accents Tom,' I said. 'You've got quite a gift for telling stories. Ever thought of being an actor?'

Tom blushed. It worked. Always does. Every time a coconut. Stroking their ego massages their tongue. I didn't need to learn that at university. That's life when you're a natural blonde. Tom stood up straight and tossed his head back before continuing. He was rather jealous, in a good way I'd say, that his friend Rick had scored yet again.

'I can't believe the girls fall for it. I'd be too embarrassed to say stuff that was so in your face. But Rick pulls more times than not. Even me mum thinks

50

he's a luv. And she can spot a wanker, even when she's half cut.'

His mother was going to be pleased!

He went on to describe the minutiae of flirting and exchanging details between the four of them. That sequence, I knew, was a definite for the cutting floor. Tom assumed he and Rick were going to end up in the girls' hotel room but that got scuppered.

'Some geezer came over and butted in. Reeked of aftershave. Asked the girls if they were ready to catch the coach to their hotel. His name was Wayne. Rick started singing, "Oh Wayne, does the rain in Spain fall mainly on the plain?" His Mum is big on old musicals. He can't half sing when he starts.
'The girls giggled. Wayne didn't.
' "Give us a lift mate?" I asked.
'But that got us nowhere. Gaydar – we were so not Wayne's type.
' "Sorry boys. Company policy – hotel guests with pre-paid bookings only."
'Then the girls left. Rick needed the bog. I stayed with the bags. The airport emptied real quick. Most of the tourists had someone meeting them. Must be nice to arrive somewhere and have someone waiting for you with a big sign saying HELLO MR TOM. Next time that's what I'm going for.'
'Well they do say travel broadens the mind,' I said.
'Yeah sure didn't know then what I know now,' agreed Tom. *'Next time, me mum says I've gotta go with her to Blackpool.*
'That Wayne geezer got it good. Sucked up to the posh family with the fat kid, the Down's one. We had

51

them at my school. They called her Tilly. She spewed all over the floor. Splashed on his trousers. Then puked again on his shirt. Served him right I reckoned. Couldn't take a joke with Rick. Poor kid though, didn't look like she was getting much TLC from the mother. A right stuck up bitch with her straw hat.

'Sorry, you'd better take that bit out. Me mum don't like me mouthing off about mothers. "Respect, Tom," she says, "nobody be nowhere without their mum."

'You know that Tilly ended up being a real star. Little blob of sunshine that kept us all sane. Playing games and singing after it all kicked off. She wasn't half bright and brave. Got permission to play chess and then whopped us all. Her mother didn't even watch her in the final. Sorry ma, but that's how it was.'

'So what happened after Tilly was sick at the airport?' I prompted.

'The kid was bawling and shouting, "Jane, Jane."

'Wayne scraped the chuck off his shirt and spoke into his walkie talkie. He was well pissed off, he was. Then nearly everyone left the building. Wayne and his lot went off in one of them mini-buses. Rick still hadn't returned. I saw that the fat had kid'd dropped her doll. Covered in vomit, disgusting. I stepped in and rescued it after some local random tried to nick it. Good excuse to follow those girls. Knights in swimming shorts we was. Rick and me delivered the doll to Tilly direct.'

I paused the tape. I had missed the reference until now. Tilly travelled with a doll called Jane. What were the chances?

I looked at my watch. No time to follow through on the connection. I had agreed to a follow up session at the zoo. Conquering arachnophobia was my priority under the circumstances.

8. Jack

I've always liked guns. Me Pa gave us a water pistol one Christmas… before he did a runner with the blonde in his office who worked at the depot. Ma said she'd like a real one with two bullets… one for me Pa, the other for the blonde. Me Gran told her off for talking like that.

'He's a good boy, your Jack. Don't you be giving him bad ideas,' she scolded.

Gran said the water pistol must have got lost in the move to her place after me Ma left with her new boyfriend. He didn't do kids. So me Gran said I could live with her. It didn't seem that different really. Me Pa and me Ma weren't hardly ever around. They was either at work or the pub. Gran was the one that took me to school, cooked me dinner and put me to bed. She was short and nugget strong with white hair (the Marilyn Monroe colour, she called it) but you wouldn't call her a sweet little old lady. A chain smoking (Marlborough Lights), tee total, no swearing allowed, tea swigging grafter, she was tough but fair. When I told her I was going to join the army she sulked for two days.

Before I went off to cadet training she marched me down to the cemetery.

'I've packed us a picnic,' she said.

I thought she'd lost the plot. A thermos of tea and marmite buns beside the grave stones were not my idea of a good day out. A group of us from school used to hang out there on a Saturday night smoking dope and downing vodka shots straight from the bottle. We talked big about girls and sex and all the stuff we thought we wanted to do but didn't really have a clue about how to go about getting it. The girls at school were too cool to hang out with anyone not earning real money. So it was just bragging amongst us non-legal

54

wannabes. Our closest experience to the real stuff came from porn sites. I were still a virgin when I joined the army.

'Time for a history lesson, my lad,' Gran said when we arrived at the cemetery. She walked directly towards three graves with angels and leaves carved on the head stones. The names said Rupert, Jack and Cecil Smith were buried below.

'My grandfather and his two brothers rest there,' Gran stated.

'Real sad they all got theirselves wiped out,' I replied. None of them was over twenty five.

'Not a brain between them left,' she said. 'Shot, the lot of them in the Somme. One uncle came back with half a head, the other minus his legs. My grandmother said her husband had all his bits but the mustard gas cooked his brain. They all died in a cottage hospital in Lydney within six weeks of each other. The undertaker did a special deal. The family paid him off in instalments over three years.'

'I'm not planning to get killed, Gran.'

'You keep that silly head of yours down low. I don't want a dead hero.'

The training nearly did me in. You try fourteen weeks of marching round and round a parade ground forwards, backwards and sideways, a fitness regime designed to kill or cure in the name of safety and survival. The team building exercises were run by a sadist with the rank of sergeant. I dug the weapons training though. Cool as, learning how to handle a rifle, shoot a machine gun, use night viewing techie stuff. Once we moved from simulators on to the ranges it was like starring in your own *Diehard* movie.

'Bloody awesome,' I told Gran on one of my telephone calls.

'You watch your tongue, my boy. Being a man isn't

about a potty mouth. Those soldiers, they'll talk about stuff you're too young to think about. You just remember how I've brought you up – respect women, be polite to everyone and bow to nobody.'

'What if I have to meet the Queen?'

That made Gran laugh. She told me to make sure my shoes were clean and that I washed behind my ears.

'Her grandson's been to Afghanistan and all,' she said. 'We've got a lot in common, Her Majesty and me.'

Me best mate at training camp was called Harry. He wasn't a royal, didn't have red hair, but he was good with guns and girls. When I asked him for advice about talking to Giselle he slapped me on the back and laughed. 'Aim high mate. They all love a man in uniform.'

9. Tilly

For my second session with Psycho I took Jane and my metal handbag. It looks like a small suitcase. It has stickers on it from all round the world. The best one is hot pink with sparkly words: PHOTOGRAPHERS DO IT IN A FLASH.
'That's an unusual case, Tilly,' Psycho said.
'I bought it at a jumble sale,' I told her. 'SWMBO won't usually let me take it out of the house. I keep my photos in it. Looks just like what those famous photographers use. SWMBO said I could bring it today 'cause you might be interested in some of the shots I took at the Garden of Eden Hotel.'
Psycho's eyes opened wide. Me and Jane knew it was a good move bringing that case and worth the argument at home. I laid out my photographs on the table, next to the jar with the chocolates. I saw it was full again. I gave a choc equals good news wink to Jane and put her on the chair as Psycho studied the images.
'These are very interesting, Tilly.'
Jane smirked at me. Game on, she was saying.
'I like photography.'
'You're good at it.'
'I know. I'm planning to turn professional. This year I've earned heaps. I got a twenty-five pound voucher in a competition. I took a portrait of Jane and won. I also got ten pounds off Jeremy.'
'That nasty boy in your class?'
'That's him. I clicked him punching a kid. He paid up when I showed him what I'd taken.'
'Have you heard the word blackmail, Tilly?'
'It wasn't blackmail, not really.'
'How would you describe the situation?'
'Jane calls it restorative justice.'

'Wow that's a very grown up term.'

'Whatever... Jane and me found out about it on the Internet. Jane said that Jeremy should pay twenty pounds, ten to me and ten to the victim.'

'Do you think money will stop Jeremy hitting someone?'

'No. But Jeremy won't do it again 'cause I reported him to the teacher.'

'Even though he had paid you the money to keep quiet?'

'But he didn't pay the boy he punched, did he? So I kept my ten pounds, told on him and said I'd beat him up if he mentioned the deal. Just like they do in those soap operas.'

'The ones you're not allowed to watch on television?'

'I don't. But you can watch them on the Internet. All the channels have on demand so you can see stuff anytime. Do you want the names of the sites?'

'Have a chocolate Tilly, while I look at your photographs.'

I took two, one for me, one for Jane. I saw Psycho was watching as I folded the chocolate wrappers and stored them in the pocket of Jane's dress. I wafted the sweet under Jane's nose before putting it into my mouth. I know Jane can't really eat stuff but she likes to be part of the whole experience. It's only fair to share. Smelling works for us both.

Psycho's face didn't move as she looked at my photographs so I slipped off the chair, holding Jane close, and walked over to the bookcase. Psycho has lots of textbooks. The titles were pretty boring so Jane and me started looking at an abstract painting hanging above the bookcase. I liked the colours but I so didn't get what it was supposed to be. I whispered to Jane. She said she didn't get it either. She thought maybe some mad person had done it during a session like this.

'Do you like that picture, Tilly?' Psycho asked.

'Kind of… Jane doesn't.'

'Why's that?'

'Jane says it's angry.'

'Well I think Jane has something there.'

'Did you draw it?' I asked.

'No, I didn't. One of my clients did, some time ago.'

'Your client isn't a very good artist. It doesn't look like a person.'

'Sometimes people find it easier to draw how they feel about something rather than describing it in detail. So the painting doesn't show a place or a person as they look at a particular time – not like your photographs. That painting did tell me a lot about how the person who drew it was feeling about something very important in their life.'

'That person looks very upset.'

'They were,' Psycho admitted.

'Is the painting supposed to show their enemy?'

'Yes, that's a good description, Tilly.'

'Was the enemy like Jeremy?'

'Sort of.'

'Why hasn't it got a body or a head then?'

'Not all enemies are human.'

'Like was it a vampire or something scary?'

'Not exactly, but it was scary. In this case the enemy was cancer. Do you know what that is?'

I nodded. Duh – everyone's heard of cancer. There are adverts everywhere asking people to give money to research so it can stop. Me and Jane have seen them on television, on bill boards, in magazines.

'I guess Psycho doesn't get out of her office much if she hasn't seen them,' I whispered to Jane. Jane reckoned Psycho was just trying to keep me talking. She warned me to watch what I said as Psycho was fishing for something.

'Is that why she drew it as a blob? Going in all directions, eating up her blood and bones and stuff?' I asked.

'I guess so. I thought the artist was really clever in being able to show how they felt. It was a long battle.'

'Did the cancer win?'

'It did. I was very sad. But I keep that painting on my wall. It reminds me that good things can come out of bad situations.'

'My uncle died of cancer. SWMBO doesn't know that me and Jane know that. She thinks kids don't get bad stuff. We weren't allowed to go to the funeral 'cause she told my Dad that I'd get nightmares.'

'People do get very upset, Tilly. Maybe your Mum was trying to protect you from all the grief,' Psycho said. 'Do you do things like that for Jane?'

I thought I could feel Jane nudging me so I bent down to hear what she had to say.

'Jane says it would have been wicked-like to see my uncle burn. We saw this funeral where they built a big bonfire and lit it. The flames were massive. Bigger even than this building. The fire went all night.'

'Don't tell me. You saw it on the Internet,' Psycho sighed. 'What was your assignment?'

'India. Mrs Watson told us all about curries. She said we could make one in afternoon activities. Jeremy said he didn't like curry. Blew his head off, he said. Jane and me crossed our fingers and offered to do the hottest ever Vindaloo. I said we could enter it for the Guinness Book of Records. But our headmaster said no. Health and safety he told Mrs Watson. So Jane and me just looked up what happened to dead Indians instead.'

'Would you like to try drawing how you felt about your holiday?'

'Nope, I'm rubbish at art.'

'Tilly, I find that difficult to believe. Your school reports and everything you've told me about yourself suggests you're very good, brilliant even, at anything you want to do. Perhaps you'll be a famous artist as well as a photographer.'

'I don't think SWMBO would let me have paint in the house.'

'Too messy?'

I nodded. Psycho had her moments.

'What about coloured pencils or chalks? I could give you a note book and some things to draw with. It wouldn't be messy. You could surprise me.'

'My drawings won't look like my photographs.'

'Lots of artists draw things that don't look anything like reality. Remember it's the feeling that's important. Not the object or the person. Maybe you and Jane could do some research on abstract painters?'

'Mrs Watson took our class to the Tate Modern. It's this big place on the river in London. It used to be full of coal and stuff and they made electricity there. Then they cleaned it all up and stuffed it full of weird paintings. Some really, really humongous ones that take up like a whole wall. Lots of colours, and some of them are really rude, willies and stuff like that.'

'What was your favourite?'

'Jackson Pollock. I'd love to do that stuff. He flung paint all over the floor, all over the canvas, all over himself. Jane and me reckon that would be wicked. Especially if someone was going to pay us millions.'

'Why did you like his work, Tilly?'

''Cause it was moving. Wherever I looked in the painting the lines were going everywhere. I don't think that Mr Pollock could sleep. He was just too busy having fun.'

'Well maybe that's a good example. Come sit down here again and tell me something. If you had to pick out the

61

people who you found most interesting on your holiday, who would you choose?'

'Is this like a test? Do I have to put them in order like counting? Ascending, descending, parallel, that sort of stuff? Have I got a time limit?'

'No, it's not a test. I'd just like to learn more about who was there with you, when the incident happened.'

I went over to the photographs and chose nine people, six males and two females. I told Psycho who each of them was.

'What a good memory you have, Tilly,' she said. 'I'll never remember all those names. Can you write their names on a piece of paper and I will put the photograph above the name? Then when you talk about them I'll be able to recognize who you're talking about.'

Jane and me thought that was a good idea. I wrote down the names of Wayne, Tom, Angus, FJ, Livingstone, Shazza, Giselle and Jack. But I told Psycho there was no way the ninth name and photograph could sit with the others.

'Yousef wouldn't want to sit next to any of them,' I said.

'You think?'

'I KNOW so.'

'Maybe you could draw how you felt about these people as well as taking photographs of them?' said Psycho.

'Why would I do that if you want me to talk about them?'

'Like I said, sometimes what we feel doesn't look like what we see. Perhaps Jane might like to put her point of view?'

'I'll ask her,' I said, 'but not now. We would have to talk about it, in private, you understand.'

'Absolutely. I'll give you a notepad and pencils when you leave today. Just in case Jane thinks it would be useful.'

Then Psycho returned to looking at the photographs. She selected one and asked, 'Tell me about this Wayne, the tour operator representative. You and Jane didn't get off to the best start with him, did you?'

'Jane said that her, me and Wayne displayed a classic incompletion of Tuckman's Stages.'

'We are talking about the psychologist Bruce Tuckman, are we?'

'That's him, group dynamics and decision making stuff,' I agreed and placed Jane in the centre of my lap, 'Jane thought you'd know his stuff?'

'It's a while since I studied the textbooks. I guess you've been on that Internet again. More homework? Why don't you remind me of any theories you consider relevant?'

I did that, with gusto. Five stages – forming, storming, norming, performing and mourning. I like doing that sort of work at school. Especially as it surprises the grown-ups. They expect people like me to be stupid. Not my teacher, Mrs Watson, she knows I'm smart, most of the time. I'm the cleverest kid in the school... for someone like me that is.

'Very impressive, accurately described, succinctly presented. I'm not sure most of my graduate students could match you. I can see why all your classmates see you as Tilly the terrific.'

'Not Jeremy. He doesn't call me that.'

'Well I don't think we need to bother about Jeremy. Let's concentrate on Wayne and your links with Tuckman.'

'Wayne just pretended to get along with others. That's what Tuckman calls stage one, forming. I found Wayne out. He told lots of lies. Jane and me heard him when we were doing our covert operational tactics.'

'Goodness Tilly, what's that?'

63

'Internet speak for spying. It's really good fun. You get to learn heaps.'

'I'm sure you do. It sounds like you and Jane had a bit of an adventure. Where did you start these covert operations?'

'At the hotel 'cause we got invited to a boring party. It was called a meet and greet. Nobody wanted to meet or greet me and Jane. So we took my camera and crawled under a table near the bar. That's where most of the food was and you get to hear everything. I got some great pics. I took that one of Wayne when he was talking about my family. Being really rude, he was. Talking to an old man called Stripey. He came from America and he was another rep. Both of them were talking to Angus.'

I pointed to the photograph of the man wearing a clerical collar. 'That's Angus. He's a vicar.'

'What did Wayne say?' Psycho wanted to know as she placed the image of Wayne beside the one of Angus.

'That he knew he was going to win the bet. The competition was for resort representative of the week.

' "Category A, family from hell," that Wayne said.

'When Stripey and Angus asked him why, he answered, "Geezz-us Christ man, score one, Tilly Henderson-Smythe, jelly babe. She's the special needs, elephant kid handcuffed to a rag doll. Spewed all over me. Score two, Henderson-Smythe mama, star export of the Genghis Khan school of tactics. She's armed with a mental checklist of complaints. And for the hat trick there's Mr Henderson-Smythe. Every family has one, best stored with the other wet mops in the broom cupboard."

'How rude is that? And anyway I'm not a kid. I'm an ad-o-les-cent. Big difference I can tell you.'

'Well he didn't know you and Jane were under the table listening. Do you ever say things to Jane that you wouldn't want anyone else to hear?'

'Like calling Mummy SWMBO, you mean?'

'That's a good example, Tilly. What else did you hear under that table?'

'That Stripey man laughed, in a mean way, and said it was start-of-the-season luck. He said Wayne should upgrade us to the penthouse. That way he'd still get a big tip.

'Angus said, "Be positive."

'But Wayne just argued, "You didn't have to clean up the puke at the airport. Gut feeling – that family is an omen."

'Angus told him, "It will only get better."

'Wayne gave him a look just like SWMBO's death ray one.'

'Did it work?' asked Psycho.

'Kind of. Wayne stopped talking about me and the rents. Angus asked him how he got into the job.

' "Nobody grows up wanting to be a representative for a tour operator in a holiday resort," Wayne said. "You don't exactly train to body bag a tourist drowned in an infinity pool."

' "Being a rep and working in all this sunshine must have its benefits," Angus replied.

' "Hey, I'm a walking first aider, restaurant guide, agony aunt, and pleasure seeker," Wayne said. "I aim to be all things to all guests."

'I wanted to stick my head out and say, you're FAILING Wayne, BIG TIME, with me and Jane.

'Later on, when it all went big bazoobo. I heard Tom and Rick talking about Wayne. They said Wayne was all things to all guests. That included... rumpty-pumpty. You know what that is?'

'Hmm, not sure I do,' Psycho said. 'Why don't you tell me?'

'It's a bit rude. You won't go mad at me, will you?'

'No, I promise. Remember – anything you say and anyway you say it in this room is okay with me.'

Jane gave me a nudge. That meant it was okey dokey to tell Psycho.

'They said that Stripey was Wayne's fuck buddy from Chicago. Grown-ups can do rumpty-pumpty when life gets dull. Jane and me thought that was just too gross. But I don't think they were right.'

'Why was that Tilly? Tuckman's theories again?'

''Cause you get your head chopped off by the Imam for doing rumpty-pumpty with a man where we went on holidays. Wayne is a bully. He'd be too scared to fight with an Imam. And anyway you don't do sex when you're old.'

'Is that so Tilly? I wouldn't have described Wayne, in this photograph, as old,' said Psycho.

'He is. He told Angus he was forty!

' "And the rest," Stripey laughed.

'Jane and me think that Wayne's got a problem with numbers. He might be special needs too.'

'What else did you learn about Wayne?' Psycho asked.

'He talked about all the nice people he got to meet. Us Henderson-Smythe's were not mentioned.

' "You might try to sound hard and cynical," Angus said to Wayne, "but I can hear you really do like people."

'Wayne agreed people on beach holidays were easy enough to like. "Up for a good time, cheerful if the sun's shining, relaxed as long as the food's recognisable and not in too much need of culture brokering," he told Angus.

'Jane thought Wayne had been reading too many holiday brochures. He sounded dumb talking like that – real rent speak.

'Stripey and Wayne told Angus how the resort reps put the tourists into tribes. The four Ss (sun, sea, sand and sex), the three Fs (family, friends or frequent-flyers), the two Ts (tossers and troublemakers), and the loner (hard work because they're depressed, divorced, deviant or all three). Me and Jane thought that was quite clever for people who did rumpty-pumpty when they were bored.

' "You have to wonder if some people should ever be given a passport," said Wayne. "You wouldn't believe some of the complaints we get."

' "Like what? Give me some stories," asked Angus.

'Stripey said his favourite was about Americans who complained about spicy food and curry... on holiday in India. Wayne talked about disgusted Kevin. He was on a cultural tour of Greece, and whinged about the lack of proper biscuits like ginger nuts and custard creams.

'I didn't really get that 'cause I like those sort of biscuits too. Kevin should have packed some, like SWMBO does. She takes a jar of Marmite whenever we stay away from our house.

' "Toast without Marmite is just not toast," she says. Jane and me'd rather have custard creams and lose the toast with the black stuff.'

'I'm not fond of Marmite either,' Psycho agreed.

'You like chocolates though?' I said looking directly at the jar on the table beside my photographs.

'I like to have them here to share with my visitors. Would you and Jane like one more each?'

I smiled and quickly took two from the jar, one for me and one for Jane. After I had let Jane smell them I ate them. Psycho kept asking questions.

'So Tilly, you wouldn't give the meet and greet party top marks?'

'Some bits were okay. Like the invitation. It was really fancy. The writing was just like a wedding one.'

'You mean embossed – sort of raised writing in gold?'

'Yep, and we got a goodie bag like at a little kid's party.'

'Well that was nice. What was in the bag?'

'Sweets. But there was stinky stuff. It was supposed to make the mosquitoes sick and not bite you. SWMBO told Daddy not to use it.

' "Locally produced, it says on the label," SWMBO said. "Can't risk it. We've got no idea if it passes British health and safety standards."

'Daddy replied, "If it works for the locals, it'll work for us."

'But SWMBO told him not to use it on me. While the rents were arguing me and Jane souvenired the brochure on the kids' club and chucked it in the bin.'

'What was the place like where the meet and greet was held?'

'It was called the Conservatory Bar – most gorge-otis room ever seen.'

'Tell me what it looked like.'

'There was a glass roof. There was this wall – all windows. You could see the beach, and the waves, and the moon.

' "Like a little smile in the sky, Tilly," my Dad said.

'You had to walk outside the hotel to get to it and down a path that went through coconut trees. There were lots of stars in the sky. Me and Daddy tried to name some. There were insects screaming in the bushes next to the path. Daddy said they were called cicadas. Jane and me read on the Internet that Chinese people eat them, dipped in chocolate. Gross!

'When we walked into the bar there was a garden with real flowers growing inside. It smelled like the perfume department in Harrod's. Even Mummy said to Wayne, "This is Paradise."

'Jane and me giggled 'cause that's the name of the company that owns the hotel. Of course it is, I wanted to say. But I didn't. I just wanted the whole night to be as perfect as that room. Even if Wayne had to be there as well. Turned out he agreed with me and SWMBO.'

'What do you mean?' asked Psycho

'Well, when I was under the table I heard Wayne talking about it.

' " Impressive, great place, great beach, even the locals are great."

'He said that in lots of places where he worked, the locals were a big nuisance on the beach. But in this place they don't flog trinkets and tourist tat to us sunbathers. There is a big sign at the Garden of Eden hotel – no outsiders.

'I wanted to stick my head out again and say, "What about the sand sweeper and the towel boy? They're outsiders, but like inside." But I didn't.

'Reverend Angus said he was worried about something called beach apartheid and what would happen if the locals turned sour.

' "Heaven on earth has different rules to your one in the clouds," said Wayne.

'Stripey added, "Tourists want what tourists want. Holidays where they can live the dream."

' "Whose holiday is it? Whose home is it?" asked Angus.

' "You've been brain washed by that Yousef," said Wayne.

'I didn't know then who Yousef really was. But Wayne knew him 'cause Yousef worked as a cleaner at the airport and a waiter at the pool bar in our hotel. Then Angus went off to the loo. Wayne started talking about him behind his back. He told Stripey that Angus spent too much time talking to Yousef.'

'Don't you think it's a bit strange? Why would a young

Muslim lad want to spend time with Angus, an old lag in a dog collar?'

'Me and Jane didn't get that. Daddy lags pipes so they don't burst in the winter. I told Jane that maybe Angus was a plumber when he wasn't being a vicar. But I didn't know what happened to his dog or why he wore its collar? I hadn't seen a dog anywhere in the hotel. Maybe it got lost or drowned.

'Stripey said, "Angus is a good listener. Yousef does like to bang on about politics and religion."

' "Yousef's a trouble maker," said Wayne. "I hope our Reverend isn't encouraging him."

'When Angus came back they all started talking about the hotel again. It was kind of boring. Jane and me wanted to escape and get some more coke to drink.

' "This hotel has a golf course and three swimming pools," Angus said. "Do you have any notion of how the locals feel about it?"

' "The locals don't play golf, Angus. And they swim in the sea. So there's no problem," Wayne replied.

' "So whose water supply keeps the putting greens? Whose water fills those pools?"

' "Who's providing jobs on the golf course and in the hotel for all these locals?" argued Wayne.

' "Stalemate," shouted Stripey, "Let's have another round of single malts and continue with our Reverend's earthly education. There's more to life than communion wine."

'Jane whispered to me that she'd heard the rents talking to Wayne about golf. That is just the most boring of boring stuff.

' "Single figure handicap?" asked Wayne.

' "You got it," said my Dad.

'I don't think Daddy is handicapped. He plays with our

70

neighbour, Mr Heaton, every weekend. Our neighbour walks. He doesn't use a wheelchair.

' "Another round of single malts it is," said Angus.

'Wayne collected some drinks from the bar. They made a toast to sunshine and then Angus told a couple of jokes which Jane and me thought were pretty silly.

' "You're as shaggible as a coconut, Angus," said Wayne, "with the only supply of clean jokes in the resort."

' "Rare as real blondes these days," added Stripey.

' "It's okay to have a resident happy clappy around who gets along with everyone," said Wayne.'

'You do a very good job at mimicking how people speak, Tilly,' said Psycho.

'Jane and me are practising. Maybe we'll do the Edinburgh festival. My dad says I should be on the stage.'

'He could be right,' Psycho agreed, 'From what you say it sounds like Angus, Wayne and Stripey were all good friends.'

'That was the first nice thing I'd heard that Wayne say to anybody. You might think that sounded like Tuckman's Stage 3, norming. But I didn't trust that Wayne one little bit. I think he was just pretending to be friends and part of the group. Like after it all kicked off with Yousef. Wayne pretended he could understand what Yousef wanted to say to everyone. '

'Tilly, what did Wayne do when he saw Yousef? Wasn't he an outsider at the meet and greet?' Psycho asked.

'I don't think Wayne saw Yousef, not until the end. The bar was buzzing. Jane and me had snuck out from under the table to get some sausages. They had those little ones on sticks, with tomato sauce. I wanted to get a plate of things to eat and another coke.

'That's when I saw those two girls from the airport. You know the one who had the dolphin tattoo on her chest and

71

the girl with red knickers under her white shorts. They had their party outfits on. I really liked what the girl Shazza, wore. It was floaty with sparkly spots on it. And you could see straight through it when she stood in front of the light. SWMBO definitely didn't approve. But fucking Rick and shitty Tom did. Shazza went over to those big boys. She said her friend was called Trace.

' "Is that short for Tracey?" I asked, 'cause the sausages were right next to where she was standing.

'They giggled and said, "Sweet. Don't ya jez luv the doll?"

'I didn't find it funny but I smiled anyway. At least they talked to kids.

'The four of them were looking for Wayne 'cause he was the person who sold outings from the hotel. I'd asked the rents if we could buy a ticket for an outing. Daddy thought it might be nice to go see the local kids at their village school. I didn't mind as long as I didn't have to join in the class. I was on half term. No homework. But SWMBO didn't want us to go.

' "Disease," she said. "Do you know those children don't even wear shoes to school?"

'I thought that was cool, lucky them.'

'Maybe they're too poor to buy shoes?' suggested Psycho.

'Then they should ask for more pocket money. Or their parents should buy them school shoes. Mummy gets mine in the John Lewis sale.'

'What sort of an outing did the young people buy?'

'Rick and his gang booked to go on the adventure excursion. That meant they got to go in a four by four car with no roof, ski down a sand dune on a board, snorkel on the coral reef and have a barb-a-que lunch on a deserted beach. Jane and me would have loved to go too but they didn't ask us. The kids' club didn't do anything that much fun.

' "Listen boys," said Wayne, "I know you're gate-crashing. But since you've booked my excursion, you can stay at the party. But take it easy with the free booze. I don't want to have to call security."

'That was a second example of Tuckman's Stage 3, don't you think?'

'I'm not sure Tilly. Why do you think that?'

'Well, it's performing – classic case of everyone in the group showing off. Boys – they do it all the time.'

'You were in the field, Tilly, not me. I'm happy to accept your research findings at this stage. Okay?'

I nodded and pointed to the photograph of a man. He had a beard and a fat stomach, a bit like a Santa Claus gone wrong. He wore a tag that said his name was Dr Livingstone.

'SWMBO said to my Dad that the Doc looked like one of the gnomes that you see at the garden centre. Wayne was playing the spot the tribes game with Stripey. Angus was pretending not to listen. They said Dr Livingstone was dour, desperate and therefore a loner. Jane and me think that's 'cause he was staring at Shazza's tits through her top.

' "What a letch," said Stripey.

' "Her bra is an engineering marvel," Wayne replied.

'Jane and me were divided. Was Wayne being nice or nasty?'

' "People's behaviour is never black or white," said Angus. "Time for another dram?"

Stripey replied, "All is well with our world tonight."

'Jane and me kind of agreed with him. 'Cause we could take as many sausages as we wanted. Just when we were going to get back under the table, I heard Wayne point and yell at Yousef, "That fucker's got a gun!"

'Then the lights went out.'

10. Jane

Here is a picture Tilly drew of herself.

She did it after we read about an artist called Jean-Michel Basquiat who lived in New York. We liked his hair and his paintings. We had a Basquiat week where we used his code word SAMO non-stop. It means Same Old Shit. That Basquiat was all part of some pseudo religion where you get to smoke dope and not play by any rules.

Tilly's parents didn't have a clue. They figured Tilly was researching modern art for a project.

Ah told Tilly that her self-portrait was just too crazy good. She got no reaction when she showed it to Psycho. All she said was, 'Is that really how you see yourself Tilly?'

Me and Tilly didn't know what to make of that. That's one of the big problems with grown-ups. They play mind games. Just because they say something doesn't mean they believe it.

'Heavens, no trouble at all,' SWMBO says to Penelope's mum on the telephone. 'It'll be a pleasure to collect your daughter as well after the rehearsal. I'm so looking forward to seeing to seeing our girls in the nativity play.'

What she really means is it's one big nightmare. Ma Tilly gets to wear a camel outfit and Penelope is a palm tree. Fitting their costumes into the car is a logistical challenge. The palm tree headgear, complete with dangling dates is two metres high. How will Tilly's mum accommodate that with a paper-mâché camel head in the back seat of Audi Sports Coupe?

Ah am getting a vibe from my friend about the f word. F is for fat. Now unless you are a Barbie Doll with a totally not-in-the-possibilities figure (she would fall over with those proportions and that height of heel according to Tilly's mathematical calculations) a doll don't care about shape.

Ah am the same width from ma no-neck to ma fused, duck feet – flat and huggable. Ma Tilly is round and cuddly. When she was small her tongue sometimes sat outside her lips. Tilly's mum spent ages telling her to keep it parked inside her mouth.

'You'll thank me for teaching you this exercise,' she used to say every time she said, 'Tongue Tilly!'

Me and Tilly didn't get that except maybe it stopped the bullying. Tilly sticks her tongue out when she wants to, if SWMBO isn't around. Jeremy told the teacher that Tilly stuck her tongue out at him. Mrs Watson socked it to him.

'People with Down Syndrome often do that. It is natural and not offensive,' she said.

Of course me and Tilly know that Tilly did poke her tongue at Jeremy. He's horrible, so it was a double result. Tilly thought it better not to thank Mrs Watson. Some things just stay between me and Tilly.

Tilly eats chocolates. Ah smell 'em.

Since we saw those chic-a-dee-dahs, Shazza and Tracey, Tilly has become all body conscious... and not in a good way.

'I want to look like Shazza,' she tells me.

'Are you kidding?' Ah say. 'She's a fashion car crash. Plus Shazza won't age well. Dyeing her hair that colour will mean she's bald by forty!'

'That's not a nice thing to say, Jane.'

'The world's a mean place to be if you're an aging chrome dome. You know Ah'm right Tilly.'

'What about a tattoo then?'

'Ever seen a prune? Plums have smooth skin. Prunes don't. A tattoo will look sad as sucks when you get older. Your SWMBO ain't going to approve.'

'I could get a temporary tat.'

'You could ma Tilly. Slap it on your butt though. What your SWMBO can't see won't hurt – her or you.'

'Ace plan Jane.'

We high-fived to seal the deal. Ma plan was to get Tilly to focus on a dolphin in the sea and not one painted on her left butt cheek.

Ah figured another blog, another response from our Bad Apple admirer might just be the thing to buck up Tilly's confidence in her sausage shape and cheer her up at the dreaded meet and greet that Wayne the pain had invited us to. There's sure to be Coca Cola. Nothing makes Tilly rock 'n roll more than a sugar hit or four.

JANE DOLL: blog bits and bobs

Attitude
Think that you can, then you will
Think that you can't then you won't

Jane is green

Eco-chic or eek! sh*t!

Trying hard to be cool
Lying back round the pool
Jane Doll is feeling such a fool
Why?
1. I don't have a tattoo of a green dolphin on my chest.
2. I'm not wearing a green bikini with white polka dots.
3. I don't have pierced ears.
4. I don't know where you buy earrings with skulls.

ABOLISH HOLIDAYS!

Re: Jane is green
<<<By Vaz >>>

Get a life Jane. 40,000 children died today from malnutrition or preventable disease.

Re: Jane is green
<<<By Bad Apple >>>

I B green with envy. U beside the pool. U in a bikini. U Want to see my piercings?

Re: Jane is green
<<<By Hate Holidays >>>

Been there, got the Tshirt.
Try some CBT – visualise your body in polka dot bikini with tattoos and skull earrings.

I can offer discounted sessions to help you feel good about your image, anytime, anywhere, 24 hour email response. All credit cards accepted.
Contact me now and start enjoying life beyond work.

Re: Jane is green
<<<By Yawn >>>

I don't have everything I want either but I don't bore bloggers. Try drowning in that pool or leave us in blissful ignorance.

Tilly and me had a good laugh at that Bad Apple boyo. Tilly thought I should ask him about his piercings. 'No way Jose,' Ah warned her, 'Bad Boy will spill the beans.'

Ah s*ooo* don't want ma girl getting photographs of some weirdo's penis.

'Spoil sport,' said Tilly. 'We could flog copies at school. Ten pence for a pic of the todger!'

Sometimes Ah worry about ma honey child. She's got to respect them boundaries or else she is going to end up in the big doodoo. Ma work is cut out for me. Ah gotta start swatting up on puberty if Ah am to get ma Tilly through those hormones.

11. Giselle

I hate spiders. Even when I was a child those eight hairy legs gave me the creeps.

I don't plan ever to visit Australia. They've got two varieties that can kill you. Though to be accurate (and as a trainee media pundit I so do want to get my facts and figures one hundred per cent right) there's only been one reported death in recent history. Still, who wants to meet a funnel web or red back in Sydney and add to the statistics?

London Zoo has a Giant Huntsman. My arachnophobia course has not made me test outcomes by going anywhere near it, even if it is behind a reinforced glass wall. Jack gave me the course as a present. Sweet army boy, he thought it might make amends. Dream on!

I didn't have the heart to tell him I'd already tried therapy. Total failure, I didn't make it through the first hour.

I couldn't believe my luck that I ended up staying next to the Garden of Eden Hotel. My university suggested it was good place to do research for my dissertation. Effectively a start-up tourist destination I was going to be well-placed to gather data and compare it with established research. Bonus that the resort was full on sunshine, with azure seas and clean white sand… great place to work in February… anything to get away from the depressing British drizzle and winter winds.

My goal post-graduation is to be a journalist. I want to specialise in environmental issues. Tourism seems to be a good place to start. Every newspaper and magazine on the supermarket shelves has a travel section. On social media it crosses the board. Whatever your age, gender, sexual appetite or idea of a good time there's a product and destination available. Bonus is that I would get to travel to some truly awesome places. Like being permanently on holidays and getting paid... what a dream.

Careers advice was not to enrol on a media course – too many graduates chasing too few opportunities. I signed up for environmental science with electives in sociology of tourism and video production for television. One of our professors, a bearded grump of a gnome called Livingstone, secured places at half a dozen resorts for students to do research. I hadn't actually ever met him on any of my courses but I was grateful for the opportunity. It was totally OTT to find out later he was one of the hostages!

I got to travel out with Nigel, another student who wanted to be a film director and work on wildlife documentaries. Part of our research had to be presented visually so Nigel and I were trying to think up what, where and when over a few pints at the hotel. Then the action kicked off. I had sent a text and got a commission before the news hit breakfast time television in the UK.

Result... a world exclusive... so it turned out. There were no other journalists in the hot spot. Sometimes you just were born to get top score!

I remember cursing before I did my first piece to camera. I thought there was a stain on my shirt. White linen, great on screen, but rubbish for everything else. I had no time to change. London was on standby. But then I realised the stain was not a stain, just a shadow. I was pleased with my khaki trousers – great for travel, makes my bum look good.

Nigel used his fingers to signal – five, four, three, camera rolling. Thumbs up, we'd crossed to live broadcast. Nigel narrowed the lens. I knew he was zooming in from a long shot of me amongst tropical vegetation to a close up of my blond hair, tousled to compliment my face shape (so says my hairdresser). I was determined to project a fearlessat-the-front persona. I opened my green eyes wide and adopted the position of intrepid reporter. Transmission began.

'Good morning, I'm Giselle. It's five o'clock in the morning, local time, here at the Garden of Eden Hotel.

'Where I'm standing you can hear the voice of the muezzin, calling the faithful to prayer. It may seem quiet in this palm-fringed, idyllic beach resort. But inside that glass building to my right, Matilda Henderson-Smythe, a fourteen year old with Down Syndrome, is being held hostage. She's on a half term holiday with her parents, and is the youngest of the thirty tourists taken captive, a little over thirty three hours ago.

'Mystery still surrounds what happened. Hotel management have declined my invitation to appear on camera. However, a reliable source tells me that the tourists are all British. They were attending a cocktail party in the conservatory bar of this luxury hotel, part of the welcome activities on offer to guests. Most of the travellers had flown in only the day before. They had spent their first few holiday hours relaxing around the pool or lying on the beach.

'One unconfirmed report says that around eight o'clock that evening a group of armed youths seized the bar and ordered everyone to lie on the floor. It is unclear if the motive was robbery or something more sinister.

'The British Prime Minister has had telephone discussions with this country's President who is travelling to the area. I'm told he is expected to arrive just after dawn, in a hour's time.

'The Garden of Eden Hotel is the largest development in this new resort. It was built with help from the World Bank as part of the effort to help alleviate poverty in a country where most families struggle to live on less than three pounds per day. International tourism authorities, NGOs and political leaders applauded the development as a positive example of sustainable tourism. The hotel was built using local materials. It's provided jobs for local people. The area has benefited from a new airport, a hospital, upgraded roads and improved health and educational facilities. The resort won its first international award for five star hospitality just three months ago.

'So what's gone wrong?'

Nigel gave the thumbs up and clicked the red button off on his camera. My claim to fame had begun.

12. Tilly

Psycho was right on it.

'What was it like, Tilly, when the lights went out?' she asked.

'Cool, better than the meet and greet party,' I said and I meant it. 'First there was a big bang. People started screaming. There was lots of smoke. Yousef and his gang had these really wicked torches. They glowed in the dark. We got told to lie on the floor.

'Jane and me weren't sure if that was supposed to be part of the invite. An all-inclusive meet and greet party, it said.

'A man shouted, "We're all hostages."

'I asked Daddy if this was a new party game.

'He said, "It's okay dumpling," and held my hand.

'Mummy said, "Shut up and say a silent prayer. These savages are going to kill us."

'I hugged Jane so she wouldn't get scared. She doesn't like the dark.

'Then my mummy told my daddy to behave like a man. I mean, I ask you, how else would he act? He IS a man.

'Jane thought SWMBO had gone crackers.

' "Hormonal," she whispered. I think Jane was right.'

I looked at Psycho and then gave a thumbs-up to Jane. She did a thing with her left eye. That means watchy, watchy. Psycho was making a note in her file. Bet it's the C word – communicating – about me and Jane having a secret conversation. SWMBO goes ballistic if I do it with Jane when other people are around.

'Yousef was the boss man. He was okay,' I explained to Psycho. 'He was nice to me.'

'How, Tilly, was he nice?'

'Not nice like old people who talk to you. You know

like they think you have part of your brain missing. My grandmother, her name is Edwina Thaddeus Henderson-Smythe, well she has this weird way of talking to me and Jane. Kind of slow speed, rap talk. "Matilda dahling, do be a sweetie and pass me the book... the cat... the brandy."

'I mean she talks to her cat like it was a kid. Her cat is called Freya. It farts a lot. Are you going to hit me?'

'No Tilly I am not. Why do you think I would I hit you?'

'Mummy smacks me if I say fart. She says it's coarse and not the sort of language that girls at my sort of school use. Jane says Mummy is talking through her arse... again... 'cause everything farts, cats, people, even Mummy.'

'You could be right there Tilly. Does your mum hit you very often?'

'No, usually she washes my mouth out with detergent if I swear. Sometimes the words just come out, like when we're in a shop or something. I don't mean to say them. My lips just keep moving and then the words are out there. If there's no detergent, I get a slap.'

'How does that make you feel?'

'Stupid! Jane tells me to keep the comments inside my head. She's right. She never forgets. I practise sometimes. Sit still, think swear words, say nothing. Jane and me are working on telepathic exchange of four letter words – the F* one, the SH* and other C* words – like twins. You know some twins have a whole secret language that they communicate through their minds. How cool is that?'

'You've been busy on that Internet again, I can see,' Psycho replied.

'I would rather get a smack than have the SWMBO mouthwash. It's quicker. The slap doesn't really hurt. She always hits me on my bum. Not exactly child abuse if that's what you're thinking.'

'I'm not thinking labels,' Psycho said, 'just interested in hearing what you think about these areas. Shall we go back to Yousef? You called him the nice man.'

'That's Yousef,' I said pointing to my photograph of him. I was chuffed that Psycho had kept it placed at a distance from the other images, just as I had told her to.

'Yousef liked Jane too. I got him to shake her hand.'

'Not all adults would do that for a doll,' Psycho agreed.

'The grown-ups said he was barking – not when he was listening of course. Jane says that's typical of grown-ups. Say one thing to your face, another thing to your back. Not that Yousef made a noise like a dog or anything.

'He told everyone he wasn't mad or a bad boy. Yousef just wanted things to be better but no one would listen to him. I told him I knew how he felt. No one listens to kids either. He didn't get cross with me when I told him what the grown-ups said. That was really cool. I can't be that honest with SWMBO!'

'Sounds like Yousef was good at talking to young people.'

'All sorts of people 'cause he's got five brothers, seven sisters, fifteen aunts and uncles and seventy-two first cousins. I said he must have a gobsmacking Christmas dinner with all those people. Me and Jane get stuck with the rents and Grandma. Yousef said he doesn't have Christmas. That sucks, doesn't it? Imagine how many presents he'd get?'

'Perhaps his family aren't Christians. They might not celebrate Christmas,' said Psycho.

'Yousef's a Muslim. But not one of those ones that blow up buses in London. He said those sort are nutters. Violence solves nothing.'

'What did you think about that idea?'

'Kind of funny, but not in a ha, ha way. When he hit that Rick, it sorted him out didn't it?'

'How did that happen?'

'Yousef told us all that nobody would be harmed if we co-operated. He had a little voice, not shouty at all. He was polite. Not like Rick who sat holding hands with Shazza. You know the one with the dolphin tattoo on her boobies?'

I looked at Psycho. She didn't react. I was well impressed. She let me say what I wanted. She told the truth. I didn't get into deep doo-doo for using language that SWMBO went ape about. I liked Psycho.

'You know me and Jane might become psychologists when we grow up.'

'Really, why is that?'

'It's great saying any words you like – fart, tits, boobies. We could listen to sexual deviants. All our Internet research would be put to good use. Maybe we could do terrorism too.'

'There're lots of areas of behaviour that psychologists study. You'd have to spend quite a few years studying.'

'I wouldn't mind. There'd be so many odd bods to learn about, it'd be fun.'

'You were telling me about what Rick said,' Psycho prompted.

'Rick told Yousef he was a right arsehole and spat at him. I thought SWMBO would really tell that Rick off for swearing. But she didn't. Jane said it was Rick's fault that Yousef hit him. She said Rick made him lose his temper. Jane got a bit scared then. There was all blood coming out of Rick's head and someone started screaming again.'

'That must have been scary, Tilly.'

'Not for ME. Yousef wasn't going to hit ME.'

'It's very common for people to be frightened of strangers,' Psycho said, 'especially if they've got a gun.'

'But Yousef didn't hit him with a gun. He punched him in the face. You know what? That Rick sat on the ground and cried. I didn't know big boys did that. He kept blubbing and blubbing. In the end Shazza told him to shut it. And she didn't hold his hand anymore.'

'Did you want to hold Rick's hand and help him?' asked Psycho.

'No way. I was well pleased that Yousef did him over. After what that Rick'd done to Jane at the airport, he got payback. Mind you lots of the grown-ups didn't think that. Mummy kept saying we had to be brave and show them what we were made of. Daddy said we had to shut up and do what we were told.'

'What about Rick's friend?'

'That's Tom,' I said, pointing to his photograph. Tom shaved his head and had a plaited leather necklace with two dangling shells around his neck. He wore board shorts and green flip-flops. The shorts had red, green and black triangles all over them. You could see him coming for miles. Tom was okay when Jane and me got to talk to him. Hopeless at chess, but more okay than Rick.'

'You played chess while you were all together?'

'Yes. I beat everyone. Jane said lots of people were freaked out. No one expects someone like me to be ace at chess. Yousef even let me run a championship knockout. I wanted to run a bet on me to win but Yousef said no. Gambling is against his religion. I said that was a shame 'cause if he let me bet, I would give him all the winnings. Then he could have bought those poor kids some school shoes.

'He smiled and said he liked my mind set. Then he suggested I should play chess with Tom.'

'How did that go?' smiled Psycho.

'Wipe out, three checkmates in ten minutes. He was clueless. He said some pretty full on things about me and the rents on telly. When he talked to that Giselle reporter, Mummy was really cross. Have you seen it?'

'Yes, in fact I have a copy of the interview here. What did you think of the broadcast?'

'Sucks! Rents said no television but I caught it on the Internet.'

'I'd like for us to watch it, together. How would you feel about that? You might tell me what sucks?'

'Okay. Can me and Jane have some of your chocolates while we watch?'

'Are you allowed to have sweets, Tilly?'

I looked at Jane. She didn't move a doll muscle in her doll face.

'It'll be our little secret,' I said to Psycho. I smiled at Jane and reached for the jar.

Psycho loaded a DVD into the player and switched on the monitor.

13. Jack

Me – couldn't quite believe it. Here I was in some place I didn't even know where it was on the map. Wasn't allowed to tell anyone where I was flying to. Top secret ops the army guy said. Estimated time of arrival was 0430. Colonel in charge of the platoon was called Rupert.

Bingo, me gran'd have a laugh over that. Same twinkle twat name as me gran's grandfather. What were the chances?

She'd call it an omen. She's always talking like that. In her terms it means the gods are on your side. I didn't know if it was an omen or a wind up but, hey, the boss is a Rupert, I'm a Jack and we've even got a bloke called Barney Cecil. Just like those cemetery headstones back home where we'd picnicked after I joined up.

I got a bit of slack from the other guys. They've all done serious time in the field. Not pretend soldier exercises, real live stuff – boom, boom and Bob's your dog. Lots of jokes about not losing your paws in cross fire.

'Why did a mamby like you join the army?' Corporal Cecil asked.

Couldn't really answer that one. I was as surprised as Gran that they let me sign up. School was boring except for P.E. Rugby kept me sane. Lydney might be a small town going nowhere but its rugby team is on the map. I got to play with them, scouted at school. Some old geezer who lived in a stately house called Lydney Park was a famous president of the club for seventy years. He even set up a rugby competition between Australia and New Zealand. The Bledisloe Cup still happens to this day. It mightn't be as famous as The Ashes but heck it's something for Lydney Rugby Club to be proud of. Our most famous recruit is Georgia Stevens. She played for England's Women

International. Not a lot of the blokes in my team like that a woman got there first. Me... I rate Georgia.

Didn't know what I wanted to do after school. There's not much going in the Forest of Dean. I tried sixth form college – total waste of time. Gran didn't like me mates especially after the stuff with the police. Nothing major but Gran threatened to gate me for a year. I did a few going nowhere jobs to bring in some dosh – worked in a garage, sold paint in a builder's merchants, laboured on building sites. Totally boring until I saw the army recruitment film at the Coleford cinema. Me and my mates went to see the latest *Diehard*. Ace movie... then I signed up.

'Right or wrong, remember all bastards look alike in the dark... at the end of a gun!'

That's what Colonel Rupert said when he started our briefing at the start of Operation Paradise. A sort of joke I guessed. Probably trying to settle us before the heavy duty stuff on mission task and tactics.

'Not original,' whispered Corporal Cecil, 'but every army officer uses a variation of that advice at some stage.'

Troops need to focus. An officer in charge must signal strong direction and cohesive action. That's what they taught us in training. For Operation Paradise our outcome wasn't in doubt.

'Dally with British tourists – you're dead meat,' Colonel Rupert says, 'but shooting the shit out of local rat bags still requires a public relations victory with no civilian casualties. No Brit civilians anyway. Sometimes I think war is God's way of teaching us geography.'

None of us laugh, although I smile. Perhaps it's too early in the morning. Or maybe they're just as scared as me. The other soldiers are mostly veterans of Iraq. They've seen their mates lose their bollocks. I'm the only new recruit in this task force.

Rumour has it that the Colonel always starts his day with serious amounts of coffee, triple expresso black, no sugar. He says it kick starts his brain, tells his gut to dump before 0800 hours and cures a hangover in the mess from the night before.

'Wisdom has it that an army marches on its stomach,' says the Colonel. 'Reality is that coffee gets your boots on. To date, the Garden of Eden management has offered nothing... no food, no coffee. I have managed to get this conference room for a briefing after half an hour of frosty negotiations. You'd think they'd be grateful we're here to help.'

He points to a large map that someone has hastily pinned to the wall. I'm betting the hotel is going to be well pissed off with pin holes in their plaster.

'We've landed in a place with no history of insurgency... not in colonial days, certainly not in recent memory. Not a lot of intelligence available for the place. It's never been classified as a potential hot spot. The culture brokers at the Ministry of Defence haven't offered up much on the target population beyond a superficial assessment of Muslim moderates.

'Women wear the veil on Fridays. Men don't drink beer in public. Relaxed attitude towards outsiders. Tourism is the new money spinner. Lots of Brit investment. Minor royalty at the opening ceremony,' he tells us.

'Sir,' says Cecil, 'we got any one on the ground?'

'No,' the Colonel says, 'no reliable information available on the hostage takers themselves. No indication of the size of any local resistance group. Seems there's a gang, no more than fifteen individuals, probably poorly trained, but no one really knows. At this stage, no known links with other terrorist organisations in the region. But that doesn't mean our intelligence is comprehensive or reliable.'

'Hello Iraq and weapons of mass destruction,' Cecil mumbles. 'Goodbye to reason.'

14. Jane

Ah is proud of ma Tilly. She may be have some haphazard gene combination but she's a born leader. Ma girl is bright, beautiful and the best friend any doll could want. Never forgets to clean and cuddle me, always shares the good and tries to keep the ferals away. Ah listened when Tilly told her Psycho about how she and Ah communicate.

Tilly thinks Psycho got it. Ah am not so convinced. Ah think that Psycho keeps what she really thinks deep inside that smooth, bobbed skull of hers.

Ah also think Tilly's SWMBO requires managing. She goes ballistic when Tilly talks to me. Ah tell Tilly it's good to keep SWMBO on her toes. Let her think she's got Tilly's life sorted most of the time. Then drop in a clanger every so often. Reality checks are good for exercising control.

When SWMBO was moaning to Tilly's dad that she was worried about Tilly's sanity and she should see a psychologist Ah knew direct action was essential. Ah got Tilly on that Internet research pronto. Tilly copied down two quotations and put them up on the family notice board in the kitchen.

No great mind has ever existed without a touch of madness : Aristotle: 4th century BC

You need a little bit of insanity to do great things: Henry Rollins: 1961 -

SWMBO was not impressed.

Tilly's grandmother cackled loudly and said, 'You've got a clever one there.'

SWMBO told Tilly off for being cheeky.

Tilly's Dad, as ever, said nothing. The quotations disappeared but me and Tilly didn't know who took them down. But Ah'd be willing to bet.

Ma girl wonder is great at sussing out folks. She can spot a liar, a bully or a softie as soon as they come into our orbit. Most folks think Tilly is going to be stupid – more fool them. Ah didn't like Psycho's attitude towards Tilly when she told her about sorting out Jeremy, that pile of pants kid in her class. Ah gave Tilly ten out of ten for shutting him up and getting paid. He doesn't diss ma Tilly anymore. Result!

At the kids' club in the Garden of Eden Hotel Tilly worked out in the first five minutes that holidays are bad news if you're not an adult and get dumped in kids club, whatever the age. We did an ace review and put it up on my blog. Best news was that Bad Apple was still on our case. Bucked Tilly up no end – sense of humour is so attractive.

 JANE DOLL: blog bits and bbs

Attitude
Think that you can, then you will
Think that you can't then you won't

 Jane and the baby Barbies

Want to know
What Paradise is not?
Then visit kids club
At the Garden of Eden
Baby Barbies drooling snot
Holiday bliss or
Want to stop breathing?

Anyone out there got any good jokes about kids to stop this boredom?

HOLIDAYS ARE NOT A LAUGH!

Re: Jane and the baby Barbies
<<<By Mary >>>

Kids club supervisor: Eat your spinach. It's for growing kids.

Barbie: Who wants to grow kids?

Re: Jane and the baby Barbies
<<<By Bad Apple >>>

What do you call a kid with no arms and no legs in the middle of the ocean?

F*cked!

Re: Jane and the baby Barbies
<<<By Jane Doll >>>

Gross... but I like it!

Re: Jane and the baby Barbies
<<<By Billy >>>

I got put in one of those kids club too. Pathetic!!! The woman from hell who was supposed to make it a fun time kept telling me to tidy up the toy box. How many times did I tell you to organise that box, she asked?

I told her to I didn't have the answer because I didn't know I was supposed to keep count.

She called me a cheeky lad. I called her a c*** and got expelled.

Now I'm 16. No more family holidays for me – ever – YIPPEE.

When Tilly and me were taken hostage Ah witnessed what ma champion was made of. First class pizzazz... no panic... saw it for what it was... got the message... kept the smile.

15. Tilly

Psycho switched off the DVD player after the Giselle interview of Tom had finished.

'You have a fan, Tilly.'

'Be better if Tom hadn't called me fat,' I said, 'and he was wrong. I wasn't bawling like he said. I was calling out, about Jane. I dropped her when I was sick. Just think how she must have felt. It was all those grown-ups. It was their fault. They made me leave her at the airport.'

'Can you describe how Jane felt?' Psycho asked.

'Alone, angry, abandoned, and that's just the A words. Makes me want to email that Tom. I should give him the porn site. You know, the one I gave to Jeremy about dogs. See how he feels when nobody wants to talk to him.'

'What did you think of Giselle's interview?'

I needed to think about this question. I slid off my chair, walked to the far corner of the room before whispering to Jane. We agreed a strategy before I returned to the chair and replied.

'Jane and me think it wasn't fair to Tom.'

'In what way, Tilly?'

'Well, like he's not clever, not in a geeky way. I know that for sure 'cause he was dead hopeless at chess. Tom told us he didn't do very well at school. He didn't go to college neither. But he works. He's a builder. He's like all those men on the telly. Just thinks about girls, parties and getting drunk.'

'So would you describe Tom as someone who has limited interests?'

'In his real life, yes. But on the TV that Giselle made him look like he was really dumb. But builders aren't dumb. You know, if they were, the things they build would all fall down, right? I said that to my Dad. He agreed.'

'That's interesting. What else did your Dad say?'

'Daddy said Giselle's a media pundit. Yeah, whatever that is. I think she was acting all girly, on purpose. Wasn't she? Don't you think she made him play those dumb games.'

'What games do you mean?'

'Didn't you see the way she did that thing with her eyelashes and the way she flicked her hair?'

'That's a very smart observation, Tilly. Do you think that makes Giselle a good interviewer?'

'No way. It's sneaky.'

'Maybe she behaves like that to get men like Tom to relax? Then they might talk openly to her.'

'Nope, she didn't really want to know about Tom. She just chose him 'cause he looked well fit. I heard her talking to the cameraman. She told him to keep the tape rolling, no matter what.'

'Anecdotes,' she said. 'This boy'll give me an angle. I can feel a major doco series in the making.'

'I know for a fact that Giselle is a liar. She tells the editor what to do, not the other way round.'

'How do you know that? Is it something you learnt at school?' Psycho asked.

'I asked her cameraman friend all about making TV programmes. He said good television was all about conflict… people, situations… the more tension, the better the result. Jane says that Giselle is a star at shit stirring. That's why I said no when she asked me for Yousef's statement. I didn't trust her to tell the truth.'

'Why do you think Tom trusted her then?' Psycho asked.

'Ugh, duh, that's easy. Giselle gave Tom cash. She told him it was a little something.'

'Can you explain a bit more? I'm not sure I've quite got your meaning, Tilly.'

'She paid him to talk to her. And she gave him her telephone number in England. I guess he was dumb enough to think someone like Giselle would go out with him! Me and Jane think she would get along with Wayne much better. Except that he doesn't do rumpty-pumpty with girls.'

'That's another interesting comment. Perhaps we can discuss it later?'

'You sound just like Yousef. He said he'd talk to me and Jane about boys doing rumpty-pumpty, later. But he never did.'

'Tilly, do you think Giselle was brave, going into a hostage situation?'

'Nope, she just likes to win.'

'I'm not sure I understand that Tilly. Want to tell me about what she wanted?'

'Is this like a test? Do I have to link her way of doing things to that Tuckman fellow I told you about?'

'No,' said Psycho, 'whatever you want to tell me, in any way, is fine. And I definitely promise that I'm not going to broadcast it on television.'

I needed to talk to Jane. She has a good way of sorting out problems. She knows what words to say. I told Psycho that I needed a moment. She smiled and said that was okay. Jane and me had a big pow-wow. And then I explained that we reckoned it's not bombs that scare Giselle... or blood... or bits of body or whatever you think would make her go wobbly. 'Cause Tom had asked her if she was shit-scared of bullets. Even Wayne wanted to know if she would dream about what happened when she got back to London.

'That Giselle said no to both questions. Said it's her job to report from the front line.

' "I'm loving it," she told Tom and Wayne, "being in the moment, the noise, even the stench doesn't bother me.

I'm here, in this world. It's all exploding in front of me. I get to broadcast certainty in the middle of chaos. Take-away adrenalin. Guess that makes me an addict."

'Jane's theory is Giselle is a power junkie. Likes to be centre stage... whether it's a traffic accident or a war zone. If Giselle can be the star, she'll be happy. Jane called her a bitch and babe, all in one!'

'High achieving people are often very focused on a single goal, Tilly,' said Psycho. 'They concentrate on what they want and do whatever it takes to get them to it. That can make them seem dishonest and unfeeling to others. You might want to read a book someday, called *The Prince,* by Machiavelli. It discusses if the end justifies the means.'

'Like you have to work out if the punishment is fair or OTT?'

Psycho nodded.

'Jane and me reckon it depends on the situation. Jeremy and Wayne deserved all they got 'cause they were bullies. Giselle was kind of different. She pretended to be something she's not.'

'Didn't your Reverend Angus say that people's behaviour is never black or white? Perhaps Giselle has another side to her personality?'

'Like in Jekyll and Hyde?'

'That's one way of seeing it,' agreed Psycho.

'I got to learn a bit about her. Didn't make me like her anymore. Jane and me aren't ever going to be journalists. We know they tell lies to sell stories. Even SWMBO agrees. She says you can't trust what you see on the screen or read in the papers.'

'Well it'll be interesting to see where your Giselle goes in the next few years,' said Psycho. 'She certainly made an impact with coverage of this siege. Perhaps she's different when she's not at university or in front of camera?'

' "She knits, you know. It's her little pecc-a-dillo," the cameraman told Jane and me. "Every front-line journo has one,' he said, 'especially if they've got an extended stay where the action is. Keeps them sane."

'He told us about Bobby somebody, who me and Jane had never heard of, from CNN. That's American television. That Bobby knits too. He's a fifty-two year old, ex basketball pro turned foreign correspondent who knits tea cosies and hot water bottle covers. You know Bobby even knitted some General a blue and white striped one to match some antique pot the General's wife had back in Florida. The pattern was called Staffordshire Willow. The cameraman said knitting like that reminded him of Madame Defarge in *Tale of Two Cities*.

'I asked him if Defarge was another journo.'

'I guess he explained that it was a book,' said Psycho.

'Exactly,' I replied, 'old Defarge liked to knit when she was watching people getting their heads chopped off. How gross is that?

'I thought maybe Giselle and Defarge were related. But the Internet said no. Madame Defarge was a character in a novel written by an Englishman called Charles Dickens. He's dead too. Me and Jane wanted to know if he got shot like Yousef.'

Psycho said she didn't think he died that way.

'Nope, he didn't. He had a stroke. Jane said Dickens was one famous son of a bitch. Do you think this Defarge woman had a personality disorder?' I asked Psycho.

'I've read the novel, Tilly. It's actually a love story. Although it has some gruesome moments,' Psycho replied.

'What's the love story bit?'

'A man called Sidney Carton switches identity. He wants to save the life of a man and help the woman he loves.'

'Duh... that's a bit dumb, isn't it? Did this Sidney man die while Madame Defarge knitted?'

'You've got it, Tilly.'

'I bet Giselle likes *Tale of Two Cities*. She just kept the camera rolling. Yousef was her target. She didn't really want to tell the truth. She was so into her own story.'

'Maybe Giselle saw the story as an inspiration to other journalists. Working in the field, show and tell what people think. Dickens loved reporting. Every detail was worthy of inclusion. Every word contributed to an exciting atmosphere where you didn't know what was coming next,' Psycho explained.

'Well maybe Dickens was a great reporter but Giselle doesn't love anyone but herself. I bet she doesn't believe anybody's worth dying for.'

'A lot of adults might consider that idea to be a good one.'

'Nope, I'd die for Jane. And Jane would die for me.'

'Tilly, you have the makings of a very good mother.'

'I don't want kids. I don't want to be like SWMBO. I just plan to be with Jane, forever... the end.'

'Why do you think Giselle wants to be a journalist?'

'She said she fell in love with words at primary school. The cat sat on the mat stuff. She wanted to know whose cat, which mat. Do you know at her university Giselle is the editor of a newspaper, for students?'

'I heard she's left university since your holiday experience,' Psycho said.

'I know. SWMBO told us that she's got a job on a national newspaper. She works in an area called Letters to the Editor.

'I heard SWMBO tell my dad, when she thought I wasn't in the room, that Giselle probably slept with the editor and aimed for the owner. Naked ambition, she said. My Dad laughed at that.

'Weird hey? Why would Giselle want to go to sleep naked? Where were her pyjamas? The rents don't have sleep-overs with the people Daddy works with.'

'Did you see Giselle knit?' Psycho asked.

'No. She was only with us at the end. After it was all over she wanted interviews with everyone. Maybe she was knitting when she was outside in the bushes, waiting to talk to Yousef. I whopped her at chess though.'

'Congratulations. I didn't know she played.'

'It's another one of her hobbies. She has an electronic game. She carries it everywhere. If she has no one to play with, she connects to her game pad. Giselle told me and Jane that she views chess as a strategy for life itself. Calculated risks, out-thinking competitors, forward planning, decisive action.

'Jane thought that was complete bullshit. Giselle plays for hours. She's really good at it too. Not as good as me, but I had to concentrate all the time to beat her.'

Psycho asked where I played chess with Giselle.

'At the airport.' I said. 'Do you know she has a whole collection of chess pieces and boards at her flat in London? I can remember the list of her best ones. Want to hear?'

Psycho listened to as I reeled off the list – a polished alabaster set from an Egyptian quarry near Suez, purple lapidolite pieces with a butter jade slab board from Zimbabwe, a French antique ivory and ebony set, papier-mâché from Kashmir, eucalyptus wood with inset opals from Australia, tin from Malaysia, a Chinese terracotta set with figures inspired by some famous warrior exhibition, and a hand painted doll set from Russia.

'Wow, that's impressive. Which one would you like to own, Tilly?'

'The bestest one of all was a dark and white chocolate set purchased in Brussels last winter. She called it her piece de resistance, whatever that means. Sure wouldn't last in my room I can tell you. Jane would eat the pawns.'

'Tilly, I think you might be surprised to know that I consider you've a few things in common with Giselle.'

'No way!'

'Let's see. You're both brilliant at chess. You both notice detail. You both can tell a story very clearly. You might make a very good investigative journalist.'

'I already told you I'm going to be a psychologist. I plan to sort out Giselle's phobia. And then I hope she gets what's coming to her.'

'What condition are you talking about here? Something from Tuckman again?'

I shook my head, looked directly at Psycho and whispered, 'What scares Giselle shitless is spiders. Doesn't matter what size, she hates eight legs. Jane says it's a mortal fear.'

'It's a very common fear, Tilly.'

'Yeah, me and Jane looked it up on the Internet. More women than men suffer from it. The website said that might just be because men are too scared to admit it. Giselle told me she's always hated spiders. But snakes are okay.

'My grandmother, you know, Edwina Thaddeus Henderson-Smythe, the one I told you about who talks funny, she hates spiders and frogs too. Her cat, Freya, kills them and brings them into her bedroom as a present. I think it would be true justice if I gave that Giselle a great big box of spiders. Serve her right. She should go to prison for what she did to Yousef.'

'She didn't carry a gun, did she?'

'Nope, but it was her fault. Giselle said it was the spider. What a porkie! There is no spider in the whole world that can shoot a real gun. That's the truth.'

'Tilly, I'm lost. How about you explain the link between

103

Giselle, spiders and shooting Yousef? It's not clear to me,' said Psycho.

'Giselle told me she researched spider scare as part of a school project, before she was twelve. That didn't help. For her seventeenth birthday her family bought her a therapy session in arachnophobia. That's what being scared of spiders is called, you know.'

'That sounds well intentioned,' said Psycho. 'Did it help?'

'Nah, she got three hours with a hyp-no-therapist. Then she had to do a meet and greet with a picture of a Mexican Red Knee Tarantula.

'That was way better value than my meet and greet with Wayne in the Garden of Eden hotel, I can tell you!

'Eighty per cent of the therapist's clients went on to meet a real live spider without panic or flushes. Not Giselle. She screamed and ran away to her friend's place. Me and Jane were surprised that she had even one friend.'

'Therapy was a good start even if it didn't seem to help at that time,' Psycho said.

'Do you know, in her flat in London she has a whizzo thing for spiders? She plugs it in twenty four seven. She's got an annual contract to have her flat gassed, fuma-something.'

'Fumigation?'

'Yeah that's it. And she's got a battery powered, spider vacuum pump beside her bed, just in case. Even at university she had socks soaked in insect repellent, citronella candles in her room and oil to put on her skin.'

'Her broadcast went viral,' Psycho said.

'You want to know something about working on television?'

'If you would like to share it with me Tilly, I would,' said Psycho.

'You have to practise not blinking. When the camera is on your face, the presenter has to try not to close her eyelids. It's a special camera trick thing.'

'Thank you Tilly. I shall try and remember that if I ever do a television interview,' replied Psycho. 'What I want to ask you is how you felt, Tilly, when you heard the guns fire?'

'All I could think of was my Jane... and then Yousef's speech. He knew it off by heart. Just in case, he said. Just in case what, I wanted to know.

'There is a famous Scottish quote, "The best laid plans of mice and men... " Yousef said.

'My Dad has a book called *Of Mice and Men*. I wanted to tell him that John Steinbeck was an American, not Scottish, but I didn't. Instead I gave him Jane for good luck.'

'That was very kind of you,' said Psycho, 'and very brave of Jane.'

I picked up Jane and held her out to Psycho, 'You can still see the bullet hole in her head.'

16. Jane

Ah am very supportive of ma Tilly's creative development. When that Psycho said Tilly should start drawing Ah was worried that it might be a big trick. Ah mean whatever Tilly drew that Psycho could say was bonkers. So we went on the Internet.

Y'all wouldn't believe what stuff gets dug up to prove you need locking up or drugging down. We found an art test called Rorschach. You have to look at inkblots and say what you think they mean. Then the psychos do some maths stuff on what you say and presto... peel off the label... nutter or not.

Tilly likes Jackson Pollock paintings. Ah told her she'd better be well careful who she said that to. Ma bet is old Pollock is a going to get rumbled if they do Rorschaching on him. Pollock just does ink splatters in colour. Ma Tilly isn't sure Ah'm right. Maybe Ah am. Maybe Ah'm not. But one thing Ah do know... Rorschach is on ma nah de nah de nah list.

Me and Tilly mulled over the drawing task. Tilly thought it might be fun. Ah love having fun. So Ah said okay ma girl, go hit that paper hard. Tilly did three drawings all at the one time, Jack the soldier man (we think he shot Yousef), Giselle (the evil witch who caused it all) and poor Yousef. Tilly said drawing Yousef with only one eye would make everyone realise how he was just looking at the world in one way... maybe.

That Jack just looks plain dumb to me. Blood... windows to his killing instincts. No brains at all. Ah think Giselle is just brilliant. Tilly got the lot – pretty on the outside, ugly underneath. You just know she's not together and you can't trust anyone who has bits all over the place to dazzle you so you can't see their evil eye. Tilly sure was angry when she drew that Giselle!

Here are Tilly's portraits.

106

Jack

He shoots people.

Giselle

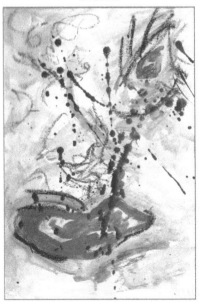

She tells lies and is a bad person.
She is ugly even if she looks pretty.

Yousef

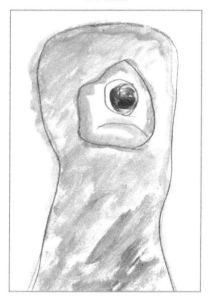

Nobody listened to him

Ah think Tilly should build a portfolio. Ma friend is a child genius. We found out about MENSA. Their website lists 17 signs of what to look for. Mozart was a good musician but Tilly is brill in loads of areas. Ah said she should audition for that television show, *Child Genius*. She'd whack 'em to smithereens. Even SWMBO would be proud.

But Tilly said we had to concentrate on ma blog. Revenge before reward is her motto. Make 'em squirm, make 'em smile. That's ma girl!

 JANE DOLL: blog bits and bobs

Attitude
Think that you can, then you will
Think that you can't then you won't

Meet and Greet Jane

Here we go play the tourist game
The tourist game, the tourist game
Here we go play the tourist game
Pissed and puke, so glad you came

My advice if you're going to be stuck at one of these meet and greet parties is: Focus on a big issue to stay sane. So my question is: If a turtle doesn't have a shell is it naked or homeless?

HOLIDAY IN YOUR HEAD!

Re: Meet and Greet Jane
<<<By Turtle lover>>>

What are you Jane? If a turtle doesn't have a shell, it is deeply distressed and vulnerable. Did you remove its shell, you wicked woman? May a giant turtle bite you on your bum.

Re: Meet and Greet Jane
<<<By Bad Apple >>>

You and me gotta get naked Jane. I be willing to share my shell with you anytime.

Re: Meet and Greet Jane
<<<By Brains >>>

If a turtle doesn't have a shell it's dead meat.

Do you know that turtles excrete salt through their eyes which makes them look like they are crying?

Re: Meet and Greet Jane

<<< By ☺ >>>

Why is turtle wax so expensive? 'Cause turtles have tiny ears.

Cheer up Jane. Go play in the sand or send a big donation to a turtle charity and cheer them up.

17. Giselle

'*Latest developments give us reason to believe that the situation has changed here at the Garden of Eden hotel. I'm Giselle and this is your sixty second update.*

'*The London press office at the Ministry of Defence has issued a statement confirming that the group of thirty British tourists have been seized by an Islamic group calling themselves* My Land, My Way.

'*Their leader is reported to be Yousef Al Achtel, a twenty three year old local man who attended university in the UK. He has sent a message. It says his group will not release any of the tourists until certain demands have been met.*

'*We're waiting for details of what these demands are.*

'*Is this group a terrorist organisation?*

'*Why have only British nationals been taken hostage?*

'*In the meantime, tension mounts. No one knows the condition of the hostages inside that glass conservatory bar.*

'*How are they being treated?*

'*The hotel has refused to comment on reports that no food or water has been permitted to enter the area under siege.*

'*There are special concerns about the health of the young girl, Matilda Henderson-Smythe who has Down Syndrome.*

'*How frightened must she be? It's turned into a holiday from hell.*

'*Will military intervention be considered?*

'*And now back to the studio in London.*'

18. Jack

Colonel Rupert seemed a decent enough bloke. Troops rate him. Some have served with him before. Likes coffee I noted. Always has a cup in his hand.

Briefing was spot on. Our base for operations was the Garden of Eden Hotel, situated at the tip of the peninsula, eight miles from the airport. Some of the task force were deployed behind the hotel with inflatables in case any of the terrorists tried to escape by sea. A marine commander lead that unit. There was a new moon, our advantage. The remainder of my troop were doing a recce of the target.

The Colonel said the biggest risk to our operation was the lack of information. What was the attitude of the local population to these young renegades? What was the level of support for their cause?

My mate, Corporal Cecil, wanted to know if there had there been any protests about the resort in general, and the hotel specifically.

The Colonel replied that due process in the development of the place had been lawful and transparent.

Cecil whispered to me, 'As if... money would be king in a shit hole like this.'

The Colonel told us that it was the same the world over.

'Land wanted, land available, land developed. Who paid who for what? Who got told what by whom? This resort was no different. Everybody loves a holiday.'

Yeah right, but not all of us get that lucky. The best me Gran and I ever got were day trips to Porthcawl. Nice place, plenty of fish and chippies to grab a bite. But the water was friggin' freezing. There was a school trip once to somewhere in Cornwall but Gran didn't have the cash. Neither did my parents although me Ma said Da had taken his bit of fluff to Blackpool. Dead jealous I was. They've got all the treats there – ferris wheels, dodg'em cars, shooting galleries.

'Dream on, laddie,' me Gran said.

I told her when I joined up that I was going to take her there one day. I was going to pay for us both, to go on everything and anything we wanted. Me Gran cackled and told me she had her bikini and dancing shoes ready. I hope she was joking.

The Colonel said our intelligence had identified the leader of the terrorists as a Muslim local named Yousef. He'd been sent to Britain to be educated. His sister had married a wealthy foreigner, Christian, non-practising. She met him when he came to the area to bid for land... into property development... Head Office in Geneva... other bases in London, New York, Sydney and Tokyo. Tycoon has a Russian mother, Swiss-Italian father – a security nightmare. Relatives all over the bloody world and at least two passports that MI6 knew about.

Seems Yousef was bright enough to graduate from a decent university. Lucky him, I thought. Nobody left our local school with anything. Not that it mattered. There weren't any jobs anyway. And nobody's sister got to even meet a decent bloke with a bank account, let alone one that could afford to buy land. Yousef should have thanked his lucky stars and made the most of it. He had it made. But that's foreigners for you. Me Gran is dead against outsiders.

'Steal your jobs, take your women, we don't want them here,' she says.

I never once saw a foreigner in our area except them ones that run the Chinese and Indian take-aways. None of my friends' sisters would go out with those sort. Our local politicos are all UKIP supporters. They get us. They want to keep us safe. Seems like they know a thing or two. This

Yousef had it all and now wants to blow it. Me I'll stick to holidays in Blackpool… when I saved up.

The Colonel banged on about Yousef. No connections to any campus organisations remotely supporting Islamic ideals. No links with radical mosques. No trips to training camps in Pakistan. Not even a parking fine or overdue library book. The model student came home with an improved mind set courtesy of Her Majesty's Government policy on education… and me and my Gran's taxes.

However, The Colonel had an unconfirmed report, (well the report was confirmed but the reliability of the witness was not), suggesting that Yousef had not been bright enough to keep his mouth shut. He's been bad mouthing land rights and employment conditions for local people working in tourism. Lots of support with the youth in the place… keen for action that improves their status and income.

I bet some of the older folks here view Yousef as a shit stirrer. The wealthy brother-in-law has bounced Yousef out on his arse.

The Colonel says he finds it interesting that Yousef was not made god father to his sister's son. The child has been christened Andrew. Not another little Mohammed then. Blood feud gone nasty?

Can't say I saw that was relevant to our situation. Where I come from you'd lick the arse of the person who feeds you. Maybe you hate the guy but you still do it. Respect means survival. Seems to me Yousef wasn't that bright if he didn't pick that fact up in the UK. He should have spent more time reading what people really think rather than study that mamby stuff at some fancy university.

The army's taught me the best lesson. No gung ho wanted.

19. Jane

Me and Tilly were touched by what people said in my hour of need. Even Bad Apple stopped being a rude boy. He didn't have to be nice. But he was. Ya just can't tell about people.

JANE DOLL: blog bits and bobs
Attitude
Think that you can, then you will
Think that you can't then you won't

GI Jane
Siren bells, bullet shells
Tremble all the way
Oh what fun it is to be
A hostage on holiday

I have the scars to prove it.

Bang bang
The Garden of Eden is a no go!

Re: GI Jane
<<<By Rifle Head >>>
Lucky bitch, being part of the action. Did you take some pics? Flog them to CNN. Pay for your next holiday.
P.S. Any close ups of the dead bodies?

Re: GI Jane
<<<By Bad Apple >>>
My babe, you need me to stroke them scars? I bang big but don't need bullets. A big hug Jane Doll, I'm hanging out there for ya.

Re: GI Jane
<<<By Pray For You >>>

The Lord can save you Jane. Feel free to
praise Him in everything you do, see and say.

Re: GI Jane
<<<By Guns R Us >>>

Join our gun club and learn to shoot. Never
be afraid of anyone, anymore. We meet
every Sunday afternoon and Wednesday
evening for target practice. Bring your own
weapon or try some of ours. Twice a year
we organise a group holiday where you get
to hunt what you eat and bring a trophy
home to boast. Your target never gets away.

20. Tilly

Psycho just about jumped out of her chair when I ripped back the plaster on Jane's head and put my finger in the hole left by a bullet.

'SWMBO tried to fix Jane. It didn't work. Jane's going to be damaged for ever and ever.'

'It's very clever the way you've arranged her hair,' said Psycho. 'Those curls disguise the wound. Nobody would ever know.'

'Jane does. She remembers every single thing. I don't know if that counts as Tuckman's fifth stage.'

'Remind me again what Tuckman says,' replied Psycho.

Jane and me worry about Psycho's memory. I don't know how many times I've told her about Tuckman. Why can't she remember?

'Stage five is called adjourning. It's when a group breaks up. Like mourning, you know what happened but it doesn't make it better.'

'I'm not sure that's quite how Tuckman applied the term. It's an interesting approach though, very thoughtful.'

'That's rent speak. Say one thing, mean another. You saying I'm wrong?'

'No Tilly, I'm not. Tuckman is not an approach I use very often in my work. Mostly I chat with one person at a time, just like I am doing with you. I listen to their point of view and try to understand how that person sees a particular situation. Tuckman spent a lot of his time with groups and the dynamics between people in the group, didn't he?

'I'm just guessing. It would be wrong of me to agree something I wasn't sure about. I could look it up and we could discuss it another time. If you want to, that is.'

I shrugged, whatever kept Psycho happy. I could tell Jane was not happy that I was talking about damage. So I reached

117

out and cradled her, gently rocking my best friend from side to side. Jane looked so sad I started to sing our special song.

Think that you can
Then you will
Find the path that you need
Say that you can't
Then you most certainly won't
Find the way to succeed

It all boils down to attitude
Focus first
Plan your move
Bull's eye
You don't get screwed
Att – it – tude

Feel that you won't
Then you don't
Start from the right place
Do what you could
Then you most definitely should
Finish in the first place

It all boils down to attitude
A belief in that you know what's best
Stand up and be counted
Be an example to all the rest
It's hardly rocket science is it?
To know what's right to say and do
Just trust your inner voice
Att – it – tude

'How lovely. It sounds like a lullaby. Did you write it, Tilly?' asked Psycho.

'It's me and Jane's anthem. We wrote it together… after we survived the big bazoobo.'

'It's very special. Thank you for sharing it with me.'

'It wasn't for you.'

'Does it help Jane to feel better?'

'Not really. She's always going to have a big hole in her head. Singing won't fix that.'

'Singing can be a kind of medicine, you know,' said Psycho. 'Sometimes it helps people connect to what's important, whether it's sad or funny. There's a whole area of psychology that looks at music as a way of healing. All around the world, there are rhythms that people can relate to – drum beats, waves breaking, whistling, those sorts of sounds. They touch something deep inside us, make us react. It's powerful stuff.'

'Reverend Angus asked us to sing. After Yousef and his friends took us hostage… before the shooting started.'

'Why do you think he did that?'

'He said that good voice would keep us in good cheer. He started singing *The Lord's My Shepherd*. We sing that in assembly. I'm part of the choir. Descant, I sing descant. It's quite hard you know. Reverend Angus had a wobbly voice. Jane said she thought Angus was scared. That's probably why his voice sounded off.'

'You've got to breathe and relax. Flex those vocal cords if you're going to hit the right note. You have to imagine liquorice, strong, pliable, smooth. That's what old Dragon Breath tells us. She's our teacher. That's what she always says before we do a concert.'

'I shall have to remember that when I'm trying to sing in the car,' said Psycho.

'I'm never allowed to sing in the car. SWMBO puts Radio 4 on all the time. Daddy likes Five Live, sport, sport and more sport. Boring both of them, too much talk.'

'What happened when Angus asked everyone to sing?' asked Psycho.

'The first time, it was a bit of a disaster. Nothing much to start with. Nobody was sure what to do next. Except Angus and me and Jane. We sang as loudly as we could.'

'So what did these others do, Wayne, Tom, Sharon, FJ?' asked Psycho, pointing to each of my photographs that she had pinned on her office wall.

'Wayne was a wimp. Squatted down beside Stripey. Some fuck buddy, he turned out to be. They crawled as far away from Yousef and his gang as they could. Wayne didn't try to be all things to all people in that situation, that's for sure.

'Tom and Shazza sat with Rick and Trace. Tom held Trace's hand. Rick had his arm around Shazza. They didn't join in the singing to start with. Shazza did later. She had a really cool voice… just like a pop star.

'I told her she ought to try out for one of those talent shows on TV.

'Angus stared at her all the time when she sang. Rick didn't like that. He told Angus to get a life. Angus looked a bit like something wasn't working right in his head… just kept staring. He didn't argue with Rick. But he did try to talk to some of Yousef's gang. They told him to get down on his hands and knees and bark.

'Jane and me thought they were bullies. SWMBO said it was something to do with wearing a dog collar. I didn't get it but Angus explained later on it was what the white band round his black shirt was called.'

'Did Angus bark?' Psycho asked.

'Not really. He started to say the Lord's Prayer but then Yousef came over. Told him to stop. Angus got off the floor and spoke to Yousef but I couldn't hear what they said. FJ came over to talk too.'

120

'FJ?'

I reminded Psycho who he was and pointed out his photograph.

'He said he wanted to be the most famous tour operator on the planet.'

Psycho had the picture of FJ beside Wayne's, Tom's and Angus'. A little apart from these three photographs there was Giselle's photograph with a tag saying TV reporter under her name.

'Didn't look like they were arguing,' I continued, 'cause Angus' body was wobbly, not tensed up. FJ kept chewing gum, really cool like. After that Angus was allowed to walk around and talk to any of us... not Yousef's gang though. He kept away from them 'cause they make dog noises whenever he walked by them. FJ went and sat with Tom and Shazza. Jane and me went and sat with Angus after the rents dozed off. Sometime after midnight, I guess.'

'Want to tell me what you found out about Angus?'

'I don't think Angus knows much about kids.'

'Why do you think that?'

'He talked funny. Not two-faced like that Wayne. Or like my grandmother. Daddy said after that maybe Angus was shy. Which is weird for a man who is supposed to talk to anyone. But Jane and me had some deep and meaningfuls with him.'

'About what kind of things?'

'I asked him did he know the story about Saint Paul?

' "Why do you want to know, young lady?" Angus asked me.

'I told him Yousef said we were going to have a road to Damascus experience.

' "Did he now?" said Angus.

'And when I asked Yousef what that meant, he told me to go ask the reverend about Paul.

121

' "Your school not teach bible studies, Tilly?" Angus asked me.

'I had to explain that my school is big on diversity.

' "Ah well, diversity is the modern agenda," Angus said. "Know the names. Don't sign up for anything. One day it's Diwali, the next Passover, and then it's Christmas. Young people don't know their Ede from their Easter. Those names are just dates on a calendar – consume and celebrate with sugar or wine."

'I told him that Jane and me think all that stuff's a bit boring. Our school doesn't let us have fizzy drinks or alcohol.

' "I should hope not," said Angus. "You're too young."

'I told him about my cousin Claire. She gets to drink wine at church. She says it's a communion exercise.

'Angus said, "That's slightly different Tilly."

' "How? It's wine isn't it?"

' "Well yes, sort of. But it's different."

' "What's the alcohol content?" I asked him. You know what he said?'

'Can't imagine, Tilly,' said Psycho. 'You tell me what Angus replied.'

' "I can see you're not the average teenager."

'Duh – that's because I'm not! I'm special needs. I asked him what he was like when he was young?

' "I was really interested in stories about explorers. Different places, foreign faces, so many things to go conquer. I rated being a pirate at one stage," Angus told me.

' "Why?"

' "Open seas, captain's rules, sun, sea and sand. Pirates got to not have haircuts or wash their hair every week. It sounded like a great way to live."

' "How come you changed your mind?" I wanted to know.

' "Middle school ended my dream. Learnt that pirates

got executed. Hung by their necks, gruesome and slow. Found out there were no places left on earth to discover. And the worst thing was, I got seasick on the ferry to the Isle of Skye."

'Yuck, just like me at the airport.

' "Did you throw up on anyone?" I asked.

' "Wasn't the highlight of my school trip, I can tell you, Tilly. The other kids teased me forever. Even so, I knew that I didn't want to live in Glasgow for the rest of my life... too cold! Now young lady, St Paul is famous for having a kind of life changing experience."

' "Like us being kept here in this room? That's what my Mum says."

' "Maybe. In Paul's case, it happened on what they would now call a VFR walking holiday – visiting friends and relations."

'I told him Jane and me had read on the Internet that's a boom area for tourism today.

' "I'm sure you're correct, Tilly. Paul was walking along a road to Damascus on his own."

' "Jane and me aren't allowed to walk anywhere on our own."

' "It was a lot safer then than it is today," Angus said.

' "You're not serious are you, Reverend Angus? I mean you'd be just as likely to get run over by a tank, wouldn't you, Syrian or Israeli? Take your pick. Damascus is definitely not a safe place today."

' "Heavens, Tilly, you are a great reader aren't you?"

' "Did you think I couldn't read? Lots of grown-ups think Down's people are dumb."

' "That's not what I meant, Tilly. I don't think there were so many wars going on in that area in those days. The Romans were in charge."

'I told him we did them in grade four. Julius Caesar and

all that. I learnt a lot on the Internet about what the Romans did – rape, pillage, real action man stuff. I wanted to know if he had ever had a kind of Paul experience?

' "Not quite like that, Tilly," Angus said. "I didn't see a bright light or hear the voice of God. But when I was sitting in the sunshine in Spain, I felt pretty close to heaven. I told my family that there was no reason why I couldn't do God's work in a beach resort just as well as a stone church in the freezing highlands."

' "What did they say?"

' "Not much. I told my boss, the Bishop, that nobody does church these days – unless they want the buzz of a ritual to get married, buried or baptize a bairn. I wanted a real challenge and a wide congregation."

' "What did the Bishop say?"

' "Not much either. I think he was glad to get rid of me. The tour operators club together to pay my stipend. That's like what I earn. So I save the church money. And in my annual report to the church council I can truthfully say that, to date, in my tropical parish it's been, in general, happy work with positive outcomes."

'I told him that sound like rent speak.

' "What's that mean really, Reverend Angus?"

' "Lots of tourists fly here to get married in the sun. I'm not sure wearing a white bikini is quite what the Bishop would like but a sand castle altar looks perfect in the photographs, most of the time. The tour operators sell the package, wedding ceremony included, with a free cocktail thrown in for the lucky couple. The church benefits and there are lots of prayers."

' "What do you pray for?"

' "That the marriage will last longer than their suntans."

'Jane and me smiled at that one.

' "Does your boss laugh when you say things like that?"

124

' "I'd like to think the Bishop sees me as kind of a modern missionary when I marry a local or baptise a child. Although I do have mixed feelings about it, if I'm really honest. These young girls fall for the charms of the local men. One season and they're smitten. Then they're back to formalise the passion. But that's not a story for you youngsters, Tilly."

' "I'm not young," I shouted at him, "I'm an ad-ol-es-cent. You're going to be easy to beat at chess if you can't remember things. Did you marry Yousef's sister?"

' "No, Yousef's family are Muslims. The local Imam did. Yousef's sister married a foreigner, quite a lot older," Angus explained.

' "How old?"

' "Old enough to be her father."

'I told him Jane and me wouldn't mind marrying my Dad. He's really nice, even if he is old.

' "That's good to hear, Tilly, that he's nice I mean, but it's against the law to marry your father."

' "Yes I know. It's called incest."

'Angus looked surprised that I knew words like that.

' "Your education is certainly broad for one so young," he said.

'I wanted to know what the wedding was like.

' "Did Yousef's sister wear a big dress with lots of frills?"

' "Don't know, wasn't there," said Angus. "Yousef described the event to me as a whoopee. His family did well. No dowry to pay. The bridegroom bought land and threw up a new hotel, employed local labour, the tourists started to arrive."

' "Is that good?"

' "It made me think of some words by a famous Scottish poet, 'the best laid schemes o' mice an' men gang aft agley'."

'Just what Yousef had quoted… but I didn't tell Angus that. I said he had a great accent. I told him he should go on one of those comedy shows.

'Angus laughed. I wanted to know who the poet was who said that.

' "Robbie Burns."

' "Did he come on holidays here too?"

' "No, he's dead," said Angus.

' "Did you have to bury him?"

' "No, he died a long time ago."

' "You ever have to bury people now?"

' "Not many here. Odd chappy collapses in the heat but mostly tourists have insurance."

'I wanted to know what insurance does.

' "Pays for someone to put the corpse in a body bag and send it home. Suits the locals. They don't like foreigners buried on their territory. No cremation allowed. It's a fire hazard and water's precious. Vital for all the swimming pools though."

'Jane and me thought Angus could offer them an eco-friendly solution.

' "Pitch the body into the sea," I said.

'Reverend Angus looked a bit shocked. I told him Jane and me were totally into green solutions. We do environmental friendly stuff at school.

' "That might be great for the sharks, Tilly, but not so good for publicity. Anything else you want to know about St Paul?" Angus asked.

' "Did he have any kids?"

' "I don't think St Paul ever married."

' "You don't have to be married to have kids."

' "That's perfectly true, Tilly. But God and St Paul prefer that children are brought up by married parents."

'I told him Jane and me aren't getting married, ever, not

to boys anyway. But we plan to live together forever. And we're going to have lots of kids who can watch anything they want on television... especially vampire movies. And we don't plan to go to church to do the communion thingy unless they give out Coca Cola. We read there's a link between wine and breast cancer.

'Reverend Angus didn't have an answer for that.

' "You married?" I asked him.

' "No, I'm single."

' "Are you homosexual?"

' "No, Tilly, until recently, you weren't allowed to be in my church, if you were a reverend."

' "Do you have a fuck buddy?"

' "Tilly, where do you learn these things? I don't feel comfortable talking about sex with a minor. Can we talk about something else please?"

' "Are you allowed to tell me where you live?"

' "I get an apartment at the Garden of Eden Hotel – part of my terms of employment. I like to think the name is a sign that God is thinking about me."

'I didn't get that. Reverend Angus said it was another Bible story – Adam and Eve, snakes and apples.

' "If we're here long enough I'll tell you it," he said.

' "I don't like snakes or apples. I like chocolate though. Did you come on holiday here on your own?"

' "I live here Tilly. It's my job. I'm not on holiday."

'I told him I saw him eating breakfast in our hotel.

' "Yes, I supposed to be easily available to tourists. So I eat at least one meal a day in the hotel restaurant. Easy for you all to come up and chat if you want. The rest of the time I can choose. Sometimes I eat with the kitchen staff."

' "What do you like best?"

' "Well I get more choice where you eat"'

' "They've got good puddings," I told him.'

'Looks like the Reverend Angus found you very interesting, Tilly,' said Psycho.

'I think he was lonely and like talking to anyone who talked back. He even tried talking to kids in the kids' club… didn't work. They thought he was dead boring. I don't want to be a reverend but his job sounded like it was okay.

'I asked him if Rick and his friends were part of his church. Angus asked me why I thought that. I said I heard Shazza say she was praying for a perfect tan when she was at the airport. Tom called Trace a sun worshipper.'

'How did your Reverend Angus answer that one?' Psycho was smiling.

'He said it wasn't exactly like that 'cause their prayers were a different sort to his.

' "Like the different alcohol in communion?" I asked.

' "Kind of… I'm not sure my God would say those sort of prayers counted as a healthy approach to faith. Still I did tell the Bishop that you've got to join in with your congregation to understand their mind set and problems."

' "What would Yousef's God say?"

' "I guess Tilly you'll have to ask Yousef."

' "Now?" I asked him.

' "No, not now. Maybe later."

' "When our road to Damascus experience is over?"

'Reverend Angus thought that was a better plan. He asked me if I would like to say a prayer with him while we were waiting.

' "Why?"

' "Prayer is a very powerful weapon in our struggle to live a good life."

' "More powerful than a gun?"

' "I like to think we can all find something of God in everyone," he said.

'I wanted to know what his God would say about hostage taking?

' "I'm not sure He'd think it was the best way to deal with a problem. But I'm going to pray, very quietly, for the souls of us all. That includes Yousef and his friends."

'I whispered to Jane that I thought Angus and this Saint Paul man needed serious counselling. Jane said I should pass on the web link for neuro-linguistic programming. Quick results, it promised.

'Angus said he had spent a lot of time debating ethics, morality and faith with Yousef. I said that didn't sound like a lot of fun. But I guess Angus is more into serious thinking than riding surf boards.'

'Did Angus talk anymore about Yousef?' asked Psycho.

'Yes, Angus said the locals considered Yousef had been lucky. 'Cause his sister married a foreigner, he got an education. His new brother-in-law sent him to a boarding school in England and paid for him to study engineering at Newcastle University.

'I told Angus that Yousef must have liked England 'cause he sounded just like a Brit to me. His accent was nothing like the woman who cleaned our room in the hotel.

'I thought it was weird that Yousef was cleaning floors at the airport if he'd been to university. How come he didn't build bridges and roads and things?

'Angus said Yousef was an electrical engineer. When he came back he had been a manager. But he'd had a big fall-out with his family. Yousef didn't agree with how his brother-in-law treated the workers. He resigned. So then Yousef had to do two jobs. So he could make enough money to live on. He worked at the airport as a cleaner. The other job was a barman at the pool bar at my hotel.

'I don't think Yousef sees those positions as a reasonable return for his time in Britain.

' "Does Yousef come to your church then, Reverend Angus?" I asked.

' "No, he's still a Muslim as far as I know. But I'm probably the only outsider he can talk to about political theory."

' "Train a brain to think and you never know where it will go in pursuit of knowledge," my Dad says.

' "Your Dad sounds very wise, Tilly. In Yousef's case that path seems to have led to Marx."

' "What, those old Hollywood brothers? My grandmother loves watching their movies."

' "No, Tilly, good old Karl. Definitely not into laughs. Share the profits, all men are equal, religion is the opiate of the masses, Marx. He was a very famous thinker and wrote a best-selling book. You might enjoy reading it, lots of different ideas to think about," Angus said.

'I told him I'd see if the book was in the library at school.

'Angus told me that he had been part of a naming ceremony. Yousef's sister had had a son. The brother-in-law wanted him christened Andrew. It meant brave.

' "I was in demand," he said.

' "Yousef's family okay about that?" I asked him.

' "They wanted the Imam to bless the child, Mohammed."

' "What did Yousef think?"

' "Said there'd be blood in the sand and a war to settle."

' "Does that count as a Damascus experience too?" I asked.

'Angus told me he advised a prayer for peace.

' "How will that help?" I wanted to know.

' "Tilly, it won't matter who answers, God or Allah. They both like you wee ones." '

21. Yousef

I trust our actions will let you hear our words. Our community is not blue sky thinking. It is sea and sand survival. So please permit me to tell our story as it is, in ways that your world and my people can understand.

The foreigners came here. They told us that tourism would enrich our community. It will create new jobs, they said. It will keep young people at home, they promised. They will not need to leave their families and go to the cities for work.

I say most of the jobs created are seasonal. They are low paid with long hours, bad working conditions and limited training.

The foreigners said tourist money and income from new jobs for locals will benefit the community. Our farmers and fishermen will prosper. Local facilities will improve for everyone.

I say that nearly seventy percent of the money from tourists leaves the area. This is in the form of taxes and distributed profits by the foreign entrepreneurs. They control who comes and where the tourists stay. All the senior managers are foreigners. They are paid in foreign currency, tax free.

Who benefits? Not us locals.

The foreigners said tourism will help to preserve our arts, crafts and culture. Tourists will pay to see and buy to own.

I say gawping at local schools is more like visiting animals in a zoo. Photographing our rituals encourages us to perform for visitors. So what happens? We adapt, eager to please you, and not our own community. Who says it's okay for you to take a cheap copy of a sacred mask to hang in your foreign home?

You do. I don't.

The foreigners said our beaches are beautiful. Tourists will pay to come and stay.

I say the hotels and crowds erode and pollute our environment. Who says it's acceptable for our water to be diverted from our farms to hotel swimming pools and golf courses that only you foreigners can use? It's your way but our resources.

The foreigners said tourism will improve local infrastructure.

But who uses these? Not the locals whose villages have been bulldozed to make way for the bitumen. It is unsafe for a man to walk or ride his bike on a road now. Tourist buses get right of way.

The foreigners said our government would be able to do more for all communities because of the income from tourism.

But that has meant little discussion and no debate with local communities about what should happen. I see that stability has become more important than democracy.

Foreigners want what foreigners want, no matter what the cost is to our community. Our voices are stifled. Our needs are buried beneath your dreams.

Why should we be grateful for foreign gifts? They bring little joy wrapped in obligation and tied with a lack of dignity.

You British have a saying – don't look a gift horse in the mouth.

I say that gift horse still has teeth that bite.

You foreigners say think outside the box.

I say look at all sides before you decide what gift should go inside the box.

22. Jane

Ma Tilly has been busier than a moth in a mitten. If we ain't working on our blog, she's been drawing. Scenes, people, you name it, Tilly's got her crayons out and her right-brain in gear. Ah am loving that child's creativity. Her portrait of us all being hostages, singing in tune is an abstract expressionist wonder. The one of Reverend Angus makes him look quite cute. Tilly likes Angus. Ah haven't met a man of the cloth before. Ah can take him or leave him. He likes talking about issues which makes Tilly happy.

But as Ah said to Tilly, 'On a desert island a coconut would be more fun.'

Why do vicars wear dog collars? I said we should put that question on our blog.

Tilly said Bad Apple might be really rude.

Ah could live with that. Tilly and me need a good laugh these days.

Hostages

We all sang

Angus

He is a reverend. He wears a dog collar.

Our blog is getting more hits every time Ah post. Maybe we should go viral on Twitter.

 JANE DOLL: blog bits and bobs

Attitude
Think that you can, then you will
Think that you can't then you won't

 Jane Doll Wises Up

Yesterday and today are VERY VERY BAD days. Everyone is talking God and god-type stories. Is that supposed to make the Garden of Eden Hotel a better place?

My question: What is it best to be – a wise

or a foolish virgin? Be prepared, take responsibility or hide and miss the action? Either way life sucks.

Re: Jane Doll Wises Up

<<<By Bible Group >>>

Jane, know that Jesus loves you. Rejoice in His words for they will show you the path and the light.

Re: Jane Doll Wises Up

<<<By Bad Apple >>>

Hey Jane Doll, you need a laugh. Where do ya think I'd rather be – in the light with 5 wise virgins or the dark with the other 5. Who's fooling who?

Close your eyes and pray for us to come together.

Re: Jane Doll Wises Up
<<<By Get a Life >>>

You want a holiday with God, go on retreat. You want a safe holiday in the sun, stay home and watch TV under a sun lamp. Your reflective wittering is BORING.

23. Tilly

I walked over to the notice board, mounted on the wall. It's right next to the chair in Psycho's office that Jane and me usually sit in. For this session SWMBO made me wear this horrible tunic. It's pink. Porker pink, Jane calls it when she's being drooby. Just 'cause we're best friends forever doesn't mean Jane is nice all the time. She tells me I'm a big boo boo when I forget to take her places she wants to go. Sometimes it gets me down. After all Jane is a doll. And I'm a person. Dolls and people lead different lives when they have rents like mine. It's no good taking Jane into the playground when the mean boys are there. That Jeremy would drop kick Jane over the fence if he got the chance.

The pleats on my skirt have been so well ironed, they feel like knife pricks on my thighs when I move. My socks were knee length, but so tight Jane reckons the circulation will be effected.

'You could end up a double amputee,' she warned. 'Get the interview with Psycho over quick. Ah can't save you if you rabbit on.'

My patent shoes were shining. My blouse was buttoned high, my hair pulled back in a tight, low pig tail. Not clothing that makes me feel relaxed. I look like I've got an interview uniform on. SWMBO chose it, of course.

'You put up my photographs,' I smiled at Psycho.

'I thought it would be useful for this final session,' replied Psycho. 'I can look at the faces of the people you are telling me about. They're good images and it helps me to remember who is who.'

'Are you menopausal then?'

'Er, sorry, I'm not following you Tilly.'

'Me and Jane read about it.'

'I'm guessing… Internet research again?'

I nodded, 'SWMBO goes on about forgetting things. Wretched hormones is what she says to Daddy. Classic symptom according to the how to survive-being-a-woman sites. I thought Mummy might be a bit young for all that stuff but Jane said SWMBO's always one step ahead of everything. So maybe she's doing menopause early.'

'Well that might be true Tilly. Women's bodies are very complex machines. But just because adults forget details sometimes, it doesn't necessarily mean it's related to their hormones. Could be they're just tired.'

'Or they've got a brain tumour or Alzheimer's... '

'Or they're not getting enough sleep?'

'You're not going to start on that again, are you? Jane and me will sleep... when we've got time... like soon.'

'Shall we talk about why you haven't been sleeping?'

'No.'

'What would you like to talk about then?' asked Psycho.

'Jane did the homework. You want to see?'

'What homework was that Tilly?

'Drawings, you know like that one up there above the bookcase. Jane and me drew some pictures, Jackson Pollock style and all.'

Psycho did a weird and wonderful number. She smiled at me but spoke directly to my doll.

'Jane, I can see you can be a good influence on your friend Tilly. What have you brought for me to look at?'

I unzipped the patent, black bag I was carrying and pulled out the notebook that Psycho had given me at an earlier session.

'We forgot to bring back the pencils.'

'Not a problem,' said Psycho, 'have them as a gift. I'm so pleased to see your art work – what a treat.'

'Like chocolates,' I replied.

'Better than chocolate.'

'Nothing's better than chocolate!'

I gave her the book. Psycho didn't say one word when she looked at the contents.

'I put a title on each page so you could tell what Jane was feeling about that person,' I explained. 'Jane and me made a list of what we thought were the most important things.'

'That is very helpful. Shall we discuss these drawings now?'

'No. Jane doesn't talk to anyone but me.'

'I can understand that, Tilly. Perhaps she might feel comfortable if you told me what she said to you?'

'I thought you said you could work out what people were feeling from what they drew?'

'Sometimes I think I can. But it's always more interesting when the artist is part of the conversation. Then I know if I've got it right or not. What do you think the artist who did that painting above the bookcase would have thought if I had believed it was a sunset instead of an enemy?'

I whispered to Jane before replying, 'That you were not very good at your job.'

Psycho smiled.

'I can see why your team wins at debating. Well then, if we're not going to talk about Jane's art work, shall we talk about some of these photographs?'

'Okay, if you want to.'

Psycho pointed to the photograph labelled Shazza. The image showed a petite and shapely child-woman, heavily made up, with bleached hair pulled high. She wore a tiny bikini under a short, diaphanous kaftan through which a number of tattoos peeped.

'How did Shazza react to Yousef?' asked Psycho.

'She didn't. Kept away from all the foreign men. She just hung out with Trace, Rick and Tom. But some of Yousef's gang liked looking at her. Especially when she wasn't looking at them.'

'What is it that makes her so special, Tilly?'

'Just look at her! That's what I want to look like when I grow up. Everyone looked at her whenever she came into wherever they were. The men stared at her all the time. So did the women – when they weren't looking at the men staring at Shazza. She's got everything.'

'I don't think I would agree with you, Tilly.'

'Even Mummy gawped. Jane said that was so hypocritical 'cause SWMBO always nags me not to stare. Says it's the height of bad manners.

'So did the grumpy old man. You should have seen that Dr Livingstone at the meet and greet party. Like he was in a trance. When we saw him standing there, watching Shazza's neck... without moving... for ages, Jane and me hurried to the buffet. We wanted to see if there were any bits of garlic for Shazza. There weren't so I told Jane, we would have to be on guard until we found some.'

'I'm a bit confused. Why did Shazza want garlic?'

'Everyone knows that garlic wards off vampires. Haven't you read *Dracula*? He was creepy too and used to stare at women's bare necks. He was gagging to drink their blood.'

'I see your photograph of Dr Livingstone shows him with a beard. Can you be a vampire and have a beard?'

'Sure, if you had a beard when you were alive, then you'd have one when you turned into a vampire.'

'Okay Tilly, now I can understand why you and Jane were keen to get some garlic to protect Shazza. Why do you think she has it all? Your hair is much prettier.'

'I'd love to have really white hair that sits like that on

top of my head. Shazza looked like an angel. And all those tats, *sooo* cool. She had a big red heart on her stomach, a dolphin on her boobie and a snake around her ankle. And her jewellery – fab-u-lotus! Three silver studs in one ear, a diamond and a dangly skull one in the other. Best of all she had a diamond in her nose. How great would that be?'

'How might your parents react if said you wanted tattoos, Tilly?'

'Very badly – but I can do what I want, once I'm eighteen. The other thing about Shazza, she tells you to call her that, not Sharon, is she is the best talker I've ever met. You should watch her TV interview. Much better than what that Tom said.'

'Shall we watch the DVD together?' asked Psycho. 'I've got all the interviews that Giselle did.'

'Can I have some chocolates while we watch?'

'That can be arranged, Tilly,' said Psycho, passing me the jar. She loaded the disc into the machine and switched on the monitor. I took six chocolates. I put four into Jane's pocket. We could share them after. There are some things Jane and me will always do together.

24. Giselle

I'm ace at interviews. My lecturer told me the key to getting worthwhile information is to get your subject to relax. Ask a few basic questions first. That gets them to forget about the camera. You bin that footage. It's usually a waste of time. Then once you've got them, move in and get the hot stuff. Shazza from Basildon was a gift. I didn't have to ask much. She was a motor mouth addicted to the worst of reality television. The words just poured out. After I did the establishment questions like her name (Sharon but call me Shazza), and what she did (nail bar), it was too easy.

'Shazza, I hear you had a bit of a holiday romance?'
'Tell me about it.' Sharon giggled. 'Every time Trace and me go abroad, I meet some hunk. I always think like it's gonna be THE ONE. Trace says there isn't THE ONE. There's hundreds. It just depends who comes along first. I think that's complete shit. It's her ma's fault. She's real bitter about men... got a bad attitude, if you know what I mean. Ever since Trace's dad pissed off with some slag who worked in his office. Mind you, you could hardly blame him, my dad said. Trace's ma hasn't half got a mouth.'

'Really?' was all I needed to say to keep her in full flood.

'I know my soul mate's out there. You jez gotta get out there and find 'im. I've been engaged four times. True Giselle. I have. I've got the rings to prove it. Two with diamonds, one with a ruby and the other's got emeralds and black pearls. Trace's ma reckons they're not real, just pretend precious stones.

Cow... *you can see what I mean when I say she's got a bad attitude?*

'*You have to think positive. That's what the magazines say. You gotta be in it to get it. So I got a new bikini, had a Brazilian, got me eyelashes dyed and booked a holiday with Trace. The minute I got off the plane and saw that Rick, well I mean, I got the vibe. Hell's bells, did the earth move or what? That holiday I saw more fireworks than you supposed to get on the honeymoon!*'

I just winked. Words were not required.

'*Trace and me,*' Sharon continued, '*well we just wanted somewhere cheap to go. Lots of sun. We like to be brown all over – know what I mean?*

'*We did Costa Del Sol two years ago. I met Dave on that holiday. He was supposed to be THE ONE. I didn't really like his mate. Dean he was called. Fit, after-shave was a bit OTT.*

'*Dave bought me one of those straw donkeys. All the tourists get 'em. Trace said it was the next best thing to some jewellery – like it showed commitment. Dean didn't get her a present or anything. Knew he wouldn't, not that sort of bloke. Anyway, he said he had a fiancé back in Colchester. I'm not sure he did – not really. I figured it was a way of letting her know that he was up for a good time. Dead cert it was gonna be toot-a-loo at the airport gate. Kind of considerate when you think about it, don't you agree?*'

I nodded. Shazza went into overdrive.

'*I want to get married at a holiday resort,*' *she*

*said. 'Romantic, ain't it? But Trace says she's not
sure I'm right about that. I reckon half the fun would
be getting two outfits wouldn't? I mean we discussed
it and all.*

'Trace said to me, "Well, what's the point?"

*'And I said, "Are you thick or what? You get to
wear a dead sexy dress at the beach and then you just
need another bikini. Drop dead sexy all over again or
what? I want a white one – like a white wedding dress
with all the back out and then a white bikini with a
see-through, white cover up."*

*' "Bit of a laugh that ain't it?" said Trace. "How
can you have a cover up if it's see through?"*

*'Nah, that Trace. She thinks you should get
married in a church. And then you should get an outfit
for going away. And then you can buy a bikini as well.
I blame her ma. She said she couldn't see the point in
getting a white bikini.*

*'I mean unless you've been on the beach for a
month, white is always gonna look crap, her ma said.*

*'Bitch! I explained you do fake tan. But Trace
thinks that's dumb.*

*' "It'd just look orange. It'd come off on your
kit," she said. "I'd do blue. It goes with my eyes and
me ma says it's a much better colour next to English
skins."*

*'Trace always comes back from the beach looking
like a half cooked chicken.*

*'I went to the travel agent and said, "Me mate and
me want somewhere hot, with a pool, a beach, good
clubs and a lot of happy hours. We got three hundred
quid. Where can we go for two weeks on that?"*

*'Well, the mank behind the desk gives us a whole
load of places to go. I hadn't heard of some of them.*

One of them was even in Africa. But I said no to that one. I mean – Africa! Who goes there? It's just something on the telly isn't? Red nose day... starving kids, Aids, wars. How can you have a holiday if there's no food?

'Anyway I said to the mank, "I don't do voodoo."

'He looked at me and says, "Haiti?"

' "No," I said, "I don't hate it. I just don't want too much foreign culture and mucky food."

'I mean I wanna see different places and stuff and I'm okay about a curry but... well it's not really gonna be a proper holiday is it? You wanna be able to veg out – not worry what you're eating. Trace says that's really dumb 'cause if someone hadn't tried foreign stuff then we wouldn'a got curry in Basildon.

'But Sanjah, he works at our local Indian, says that English curry ain't nothin' like what you get in India. I'm not sure he's telling the truth. Trace says he's a Paki. But he was born here. So what would he know? His favourite dish is pizza. AND he likes white girls. But none of us go round with him. He ain't got an XR3 with quadrophonic stereo like Dean had. And he can't dance. Besides he wears one of those thing-a-me-jigs on his head. I mean everybody knows that they don't take them off even when they have a shower. Trace dared me to go out with him and get his head gear off. I didn't go. I was not back on the scene just then. That bastard Dave hadn't called me. Like he promised. So he didn't turn out to be THE ONE. Just another shit in the queue.

'Anyway, the travel agent gave us a really good deal. Newish resort he said. Only two seasons old. And a four star hotel with breakfast included and airport transfers to AND from the hotel.

'When me and Trace went to that Greek island place, they didn't tell us we had to get from the airport to the frigging island and then to the hotel all on our own. Well what a hassle that turned out to be. Changing money, buses, taxis, ferries – not one person would speak to us in English! I mean we're the tourists. We're spending the dosh. And all those manky Greek guys. Don't get me wrong, they were fit. But it was just too much... never again.

'So I said to the travel agent, "We don't do public transport. Meet and greet or we're not interested."

'So he says, we should go to this place. So we did.

'First thing I did after we got set free and were still breathing was ring me ma – boy what a story and a half.

'Me ma said, "It was just your own little 9/11. You should do Blackpool next year, with me." '

'But how can you get a tan in Blackpool?' I shook my head.

'No answer to that, is there?' Shazza asked me.

I smiled just as she announced, 'That's it – turban – that's what it's named. I remembered. Turban – Sanjah wears one of them on his head. I wonder if they wear white turbans at their weddings? Do ya know, Giselle? You're a journalist.'

25. Jack

The Colonel estimates our exercise can be executed and resolved within eight hours. He writes the objectives on a piece of paper pinned to the wall. They are to:

- bring all the hostages out alive
- restore order
- return to business as usual
- ship out as soon as feasible.

He says it'll be a bonus if we capture Yousef and his gang alive.

Me mate, Cecil, reckons that's a load of bullshit.

'The British Government won't want a show trial. Whacking the bastards shows we've got the best army around. Plus it's all in support for the global war on terrorism.'

I thought that was pretty cynical. But Cecil reckons our Colonel wants to play his part given the current cuts-to-the-army policy.

'There won't be no tears in Whitehall if Yousef and his boys get shot in the process,' Cecil tells me. 'Benefits will be no messy exposure, no Guantanamo comebacks, less expense. Bury the bastards on the island, some good conduct medals for us, a promotion for old Colonel Rupert here.'

'You think this place will recover?' I ask Cecil.

'Sure it will. Cheap holiday destination will be back on the map ready to sell next winter. Sun desperate travellers rejoice in victory. Hey ho, a five star outcome all round.'

I tell Cecil I don't reckon my Gran would set foot outside Swansea after this. He laughs and says we should treat the whole mission as a good training exercise for the next big thing.

The Colonel gives us the order, 'In the next hour get to

grips with logistics and your personal equipment. It won't be a holiday. We need to get in there and do what needs to be done. Avoid shooting women and children, theirs or ours. EDT is 0630.'

Corporal Cecil and I salute and leave to find some coffee. That's when I bumped into her. Totally gorgeous, like an angel in Paradise I thought.

She smiled at me. I couldn't think what to say. No babe that hot ever smiled like that at me, whether they were bladdered or sober. I blushed.

'Hello soldier boy,' she said, 'I'm Giselle. Do you come here often?'

26. Tilly

Psycho switched off the DVD.

'I can understand why you said that Shazza might not like foreign men,' she said.

'Wasn't she so cool?' I replied. 'Shazza talks like she's the boss lady. Bet no one ever bullied her at school.'

'I'm interested in hearing your views on what makes a person cool, Tilly. Can you give me some examples of how Shazza was cool? Was it the way she looked? Or was it more how she behaved?'

I looked at Jane. She had pursed lips, like she was deep in thought. I whispered into her ear for advice. Then I looked directly at Psycho and said, 'If everyone notices you then you're cool. Cool girls get looked at all the time. Like girls who have long blonde hair or big hair, girls who have tattoos or wear high heels, girls who wear tight jeans and little tops with their boobies hanging out, girls with blue eyes – those girls get looked at. Girls who are fat with Mosaic Down's don't get looked at. Well they get looked at but not cool type of looks.

'Shazza looked great. She acted super cool. Anything that Rick and Tom could do, she did. Like the game, Hour of Power.'

'I'm not familiar with that one, Tilly. How does the game work?'

'Well Rick said that you had to try and drink a drink a minute for 60 minutes.

'First one to puke or pass out was a loser. How cool was that? Jane and me reckon we could have won if the coke was free.'

'Did Shazza drink more than the boys?' asked Psycho.

'I don't know. I wasn't allowed to stay. Mummy pulled me away.'

' "Heavens," SWMBO said, "I didn't think we'd have to put up with this sort of going-on."

'She went off to complain to that Wayne, the horrible tour rep.

'I asked Daddy if Shazza was going to be sick.

' "Probably," he said.

'But she wasn't. And then Rick said if anyone burped they had to do a forfeit.

' "Wanna see a tattoo," he said.

' "I'll show you mine, if you show me yours," that Shazza said.

'They all tried making noises. Really loud ones. Rick even farted. Nobody told them off. Cool hey?

'I asked Daddy if I could go to the big girls' club when I've growed up.

' "Possibly," he said, "but don't tell your mum I said so."

'The next time they did a forfeit, Rick said he wouldn't mind a swim in the sea.

' "Didn't bring me bikini," said Trace.

'Me and Jane neither... not that I've got a bikini... yet. Jane wants a silver one.

'Then the boys started shouting, "Take them off, off, off."

'Mummy came back with Wayne. She looked really cross.

'Wayne said, "Now boys and girls. This looks like fun. But maybe not quite right for this place – families and all that."

' "Fuck families!" said Rick.

'Me and Jane thought SWMBO would go into mega melt.

' "I can point you in the right direction for a good party,' Wayne replied. 'Wet t-shirt competition?"

' "Hour of Power, here we come," said Rick.

'I didn't hear anymore 'cause SWMBO dragged Daddy and me and Jane off to the other side of the room. Bet Rick was sorry he didn't go right then.'

'That's life sometimes,' agreed Psycho. 'You always wonder what would have happened if you'd done something earlier or later. Bit like telling jokes they say. It's all in the timing.'

'That Shazza had some wicked jokes. I told her about Dr Livingstone and that Jane and me thought he was a vampire.

' "Garlic, you need garlic," I said.

' "Ta Tilly, don't you worry about the old gnome. Just wait till Edward and Bella drop in."

'Can you believe it? She even knows the Twilight vampires! I told her I had some really good jokes. Do you want to hear them?'

'Why not? I don't think I know too many of those,' said Psycho.

'What does a vampire fear most? Tooth decay.

'What kind of boats do vampires own? Blood vessels.

'What's it like to be kissed by a vampire? A pain in the neck.

'What do vampires think of blood transfusions? New-fangled rubbish.

'Want to neck with your vampire? Love bites forever.'

'I've got one for you, Tilly,' said Psycho. 'What kind of dog did Dracula have? A blood hound.'

'Not bad, but not as cool as Shazza's. I said to her, we should go on Twitter. We could call it Suckers.

'Shazza clapped and said, "Great team, you and that doll. Why don't you go spook the old guy. I've got a great idea."

'And then she whispered to me what to say. Didn't sound that great to me and Jane. But it worked, big time.'

'What did you say to him?' Psycho asked.

'Doctor Livingstone, I presume, ho, ho, ho.'

I winked at Shazza after I said it. She cracked up. He went spare... curled his lip... went red in the face. Jane thought he was going to drop dead, right there in front of us. No way I was going to do CPR on a hairy vampire, I can tell you.

'It's a very famous name,' said Psycho.

'Yeah, Reverend Angus explained later about the real Dr Livingstone. Said he came from Scotland, like Angus and that our Livingstone was more an academic sociopath than an intrepid explorer.

'Jane and me didn't know what an acada-socio whatever was but it sounded like a really serious disease. After Dr L calmed down I asked him why he was angry at what I said.

'He explained and then added, "If I had a pound for every time someone uttered 'Dr Livingstone I presume' I'd be a wealthy man."

'I told him that the situation was changing 'cause no one young knew anything about any Livingstones.

' "Sums up modern education," he said.

'Later, when I had a game of chess with our Dr L I asked him what sociopath meant.

' "That what they told you I am?" he asked.

' "Don't know what it means," I said. "Are you?"

'I thought it was a kind of job but he said, "I've been called that before. It's not accurate or informed. Sociopath, in the correct sense of the term, is a misuse of the generic category, antisocial personality disorder. Two of my former PhD students (both women I might add) complained to the university authorities that my supervision of their research was compromised by my inappropriate interaction, or lack thereof. In support of their case they cited ICD-10 from the

World Health Organisation's classification of diseases and related health problems. Do you know there are seven characteristics listed?"

'I didn't have a clue what he was yabbering about. Then Dr L named all seven and gave a one line description. I still didn't get what a sociopath was. Worse kind of rent speak Jane and me had ever suffered. I asked him what happened about the complaint.

' "Refuted the lot on the grounds of irrelevance," he said. "I wanted to laugh but gender politics are a tricky area in these days of political correctness. Why should I empathise with students who demonstrate incompetence? Who wouldn't get frustrated, and possibly impatient, with low calibre research? Why would I not blame others when they fail to deliver drafts on time? And as for the charge of incapacity to maintain enduring relationships and an irresponsible disregard for social norms, I'm an academic not a party planner."

'I still couldn't understand anything. Neither did Jane.

' "Off the wall," she whispered. "Harmless but bonkers."

'It was clear that he was very grumpy when he had to deal with other people. Bit like SWMBO when she has the gas board people in our house. They've got beards too.

' "I simply don't like people in my space. I especially don't like women," Dr L said.

'I didn't think women would like him either but I just said, "How come?"

' "They smell."

'I asked him if he meant they were dirty or was it stuff like perfume and hand cream.

' "Usually it's perfume. It offends me. They witter about their feelings. Who cares? They digress, too much detail. They talk in those high pitched tones. I find it painful."

' "What about your mother, Dr Livingstone? Did you like her?" I asked him.

152

' "What are you? Some kind of mini shrink?" he snapped.
'I told him I didn't like some women either sometimes, like my mother.

'He said, "My mother exhibited the same list of defects, when she was alive. Ditto gay men. I watch them around my campus. They display the most exaggerated forms of these female characteristics. Gender benders, shave my beard!"

'I asked him about his job. He said he was a kind of teacher for grown-ups. He doesn't really like them. He doesn't like field research much either, but he has to do it. I told him I totally got that, 'cause I wouldn't like going out to fields every day with grown-ups I didn't like. Especially if they smelled or talked too much about boring stuff... like Dr L... like boys in general, but I didn't say that to him. Jane and me just like researching on our own.

' "My work is watching people and how they behave. I'm not interested in an individual," he replied, "not like psychologists and sociologists. I don't get my kicks in that direction."

'I told him I didn't play football either and that no fat people ever got picked first for a team. I asked him what he did like doing.

' "I study groups of people interacting with their environments, natural, constructed and adopted. Lots of people, lots of groups, lots of environments," he said. "Nothing more satisfying than loading data into the computer and extracting the numbers. My analysis indicates the trends and directions for development. I did my doctorate in a branch of political economics. Accurate measurement and rigorous analysis determine sound outcomes and reliable strategies."

'I told him Jane and me were fab-u-lotus too, at counting. I'm not sure he heard us 'cause he just kept banging on and on about stuff we didn't get.

' "If only my moaning dimwits would keep that in mind. But half of them come from anthropology. What can you expect from a discipline that traces its roots to a handful of misfits who lived in huts in the jungle for too long? Talking to one tribe up the Nile doesn't make you an expert in global communication."

' "Jane and me haven't been to Egypt," I told him, "but we've read about it. Do you find anthropology only in Egypt? Is it in the pyramids?"

' "No, Tilly," he sighed, "anthropologists work everywhere, unfortunately. That is not to say that I don't find some of their literature of interest in my own research. Take Arnold van Gennep, the French positive anthropologist. Are you familiar with his name?"

' "No, we haven't done him yet at school. I don't do French until next year. The rents say I should do Chinese. Useful when we're all forced to eat humble duck. That's what SWMBO said."

' "I found van Gennep's *Rites of Passage* provided the best examples of the theory of liminality. Published in 1908, still a seminal text as far as I'm concerned."

'I finally gave it to him straight that Jane and me couldn't follow. So he tried to explain.

' "Well take the first part of this Garden of Eden meet and greet," he said. "I was fascinated to see what amounted to a text book presentation of van Gennep's stages one (what happens when people are taken out of their normal environment) and two (their reaction to new environments where they may well exhibit marginal or liminal behaviour). Of course I won't get to observe stage three when you all return to your place of origin but I could make an educated guess. Choose somebody Tilly."

'I thought he sounded like a complete nutter. If it had been a movie, the doctors would have come through the door and tied him to a trolley. Then they would have given him a big needle and locked him up. I didn't want to tell

154

him that just in case he was a vampire. So I pointed to Shazza and her group. I knew she wasn't scared of anyone.

' "The chances of that female forming a meaningful bond with either of her targets (white males, under 25, acting single) is poor. Opportunistic rutting ritual is a more accurate description – classic Van Gennep. Understand, child?"

'Nope! I think he meant Rick and Tom. I could see why nobody wanted to hang round with our Dr L. Dead boring he was, a real nerd and what was totally sad was he didn't even know it.

' "What about him?" I said to Dr L, pointing to Wayne. "Can you liminal him? I don't mind if it hurts 'cause he was mean to Jane."

' "The queer tour operator? I saw him watching me as he sucked booze at the bar. He and his mate will have assumed I'm some sort of desperate pervert. Probably labelled me as the sad loner on a winter break."

'I wanted to say well why wouldn't they? You have been ogling Shazza's boobies all night. Instead I asked, "Where do you go on holidays, Dr Livingstone?"

' "Don't do holidays. The thought of morphing into a lobster after two weeks on a sun bed when I could be home in familiar surroundings, producing something worthwhile, is an anathema."

'Gobbleydook – sea food and a disease called asthma. Maybe he was going to morph into a vampire? I asked him if he was here just to do research.

' "Good research is underpinned by accurate and comprehensive field work," he replied. "My commission is to study sample populations of tourists arriving at the award winning Garden of Eden Hotel. Funding was provided by the World Tourism Organisation. That's a United Nations department, young lady. My methodology will form part of a larger report, the focus of which will be the economic

155

impacts on local populations using sustainable tourism development strategies as a poverty alleviation strategy."

'Another lecture – Jane gave up and started snoring. I asked him if that was a good thing to be doing.

' "Riveting stuff, Tilly. It will enhance my international profile. It's a critical study, entrusted to me, done my way. Doesn't get any better. This little episode is the final straw. It's going to delay the whole project, damned dissidents. I had a gutful when I arrived. Nearly had my computer stolen by immigration."

' "Me too," I told him. "Jane got kidnapped."

' "Disgrace," Dr L said but I knew he wasn't talking about Jane. "I got strip-searched."

'Jane whispered that she felt sorry for the customs people. Fancy having to look at Dr L's hairy butt and willy!

' "They went through everything in my suitcase. Do I look like a terrorist? I'm an expert in tourism development not a guerrilla with a nuclear missile."

'Jane and me thought Dr L did look like Osama bin Laden, only fatter. But 'cause we were worried that he'd explode if we said the truth, I told him it was probably because he had a beard, travelled with a computer and said he wasn't on holidays. I also thought that if he answered the questions at the airport in that gobbledegook language, then they probably did think he was totally off the planet.

'But I said, "Maybe they just didn't understand what you were saying?"

' "Interpretations of intertextuality in non-literate cultures," he replied. "Bloody primitives."

' "Point made," Jane whispered. "The man's a complete nutter."

'Jane and me couldn't believe when we found out later that Giselle was one of his students. It explained a lot about both of them!'

27. Giselle

Jack was so sweet, kitted out in his combat uniform, looking at me with those puppy dog eyes. An adoring, straight, fit male – what's not to like? I gate-crashed the area where the troops were drinking coffee although their boss, Colonel Rupert with the double-barrelled surname and snooty sneer made it clear I wasn't welcome. Especially when I told him I was press. He wanted to see my pass. So I had to come clean and tell him I was actually a student. But I explained that I had contacted London and got a commission to report on the situation. And that one of my lecturers, Dr Livingstone was a hostage. How was that for a connection?

My charm and blonde curls didn't cut it with the Colonel. I think he would rather have sat among dead fish than talk to me.

'Keep out of the way. And my men are off limits for interviews,' he warned.

He was in for a surprise. I'd already found my willing and able confidant. Jack winked when the Colonel left my side. Too easy!

The developments in the Garden of Eden hostage situation caught us all by surprise. Suddenly a very large message got stuck on the glass door of the Conservatory Bar. It was hand written in capitals.

TILLY WINS CHESS CHAMPIONSHIP.

I wasn't sure what to make of this information.

'Is it a hoax?' I asked Jack. 'Or some sort of coded message?'

He didn't know. Colonel Rupert wouldn't comment and told me to scram. I recorded it on my mobile and send it to London before the Colonel could interfere. Nigel, my fellow student, wannabe film director, could do an interview with me to camera as soon as old, stiff-upper-lipped Rupert was out of the room. Maybe I could persuade Jack to say something. All that testosterone would look great on screen.

I had some questions to answer. Was the Tilly mentioned on the door sign the same person as Matilda Henderson-Smythe, the teenager with Down's? Could those sort of people even play chess? Definitely seemed a possibility when I got the hotel manager to confirm that board games, including an unspecified number of chess sets, had been made available in the bar, for use by guests and their children.

I rehearsed in my head how to start the broadcast. Something like "Expect the unexpected" gave just enough mystery and drama, I figured.

28. Tilly

'Do you know Dr L had to pay one hundred pounds to the customs man?' I asked Psycho.

'Did he explain why?' she replied.

'A technology clearance tax,' he said.

'When I asked Daddy about why Dr L had to pay 'cause I didn't have to with my iPad, he said Dr L had been done.

'Jane and me reckoned it wouldn't be smart to tell Dr L he'd been ripped off. Jane said it was like a kind of charity. Dr L's donation would probably feed the family of the customs officer for a month.

'Poor old Dr Livingstone, he needed to get a life, don't you think? And lots of counselling. Maybe he could do some sessions with Angus? Maybe you could talk to them about Tuckman? Storming and norming categories? A big boys' bonding session? Fucking Rick and shitty Tom, even Wayne and FJ might join in?'

'It's an interesting idea,' Psycho agreed. 'I could call it post-Traumatic Stress Disorder retreats. Eat chocolate and talk to Tilly.'

'We could have our very own website. NO BEHAVIOUR TOO DEVIANT. FJ could help us. We could have special codes that nobody but you, me and Jane could crack. Not vampires, not nutters, not the media even. And we could wear a uniform that made us famous, like Catwoman. With our hair done like Shazza and a tattoo on our bums saying ATTITUDE. Fab-u-lotus hey?'

I felt Jane nudging me. She was well up for the work.

'You've certainly got some original ideas for me to consider, Tilly. You mentioned FJ. Is this his photograph? It shows him wearing combat gear,' said Psycho.

'Yes, FJ wore that stuff all the time. Bit of a swiz 'cause he's never been in the army.'

159

'Live the brand,' he said.

'Bit of a poseur, hey? Just typical of boys. They think looking tough is cool. Jane and me think it's a joke.'

'You didn't rate FJ?'

'He was okay.'

'How okay? On a scale of one to ten.'

'Wayne would be a ten minus, same as that Jeremy at my school, Tom an eight, Angus six and FJ is a five. Okay even though he's a man. He was more switched on than most of the others when he talked to me and Jane.'

'In what way do you mean, switched on?'

'Like he didn't have one of those talk-to-kids voices. Maybe that's because FJ and me both have rents with issues. In my house it's my mum who needs therapy. In FJ's it's his dad who's the power freak. I rate FJ as a leader. I guess he got that from his dad. And FJ gave me some really good examples of what to do with kids at school.'

'What sort of things has he inspired you to try?' Psycho asked.

'Nothing bad, if that's what you mean. But it's kind of secret 'cause it involves money.'

'I didn't mean to imply anything, Tilly, good or bad – just interested as ever.'

'Poke your eye and hope to die.'

'Tilly, I keep promising that whatever you say to me in this room, stays in this room,' said Psycho.

'But you could steal FJ's idea. That wouldn't be fair 'cause he'd lose out,' I argued.

'I promise you I haven't got time to try and earn my living any other way than being a psychologist. Sounds like you're more likely to use his ideas than me.'

'That'd be okay. He said I was a natural. And I could try out any of his ideas that I wanted. First of all I'm going to have to do something about my name. T then H hyphen

S, TH-S. Tilly Henderson-Smythe is not a starter if you want to build a business. Brand is everything, he told me and Jane. Got to appeal to the masses with money. Double barrel names are a no go. Plus the rents would go ape just like FJ's dad.'

'I'm lost. Why did FJ's dad get angry with him about his business?' asked Psycho.

''Cause it all started when FJ won Young Entrepreneur of the Year. His father was well chuffed to see FJ's photograph on the front page of their local newspaper. He was so not pleased to see him called FJ in the article they wrote.

' "Son, your name is Frederick, after your great, great, great grandfather," FJ's father said. "The eldest son in every generation of our family has always been christened Frederick. And is always referred to as Frederick."

' "I'll attempt to live up to my reputation. You won Dad," FJ said.

' "What are you talking about?" his dad asked.

' "Peace keeper, that's what Frederick means. So in this situation, in this room, I'm Frederick."

'When his father left the room, FJ turned to his mother and winked, "Outside these walls, the truce is over. I just answer to FJ."

'FJ's father viewed education as the key to success in adult life, just like my rents – boring,' I told Psycho.

'Does FJ think education is a waste?' she asked me.

'Nope, course not. He just thinks that education has lots of interpretations. Jane and me agree with him. FJ's dad was just like my rents. They see it as public school and university. Not that anyone thinks a kid with Down's is ever going to get to university. FJ thinks that's a piss poor use of time.'

He said, 'Reading infinite books for too many years in

order to get a piece of embossed paper certifying that you've read all the books is barking. School teaches you to read, write and add up. Tilly, real learning is something you do, out of school. Slogging and slurping with money-making activities is a much better use of your energies and interests.'

I told Psycho that FJ had won the entrepreneurial award for setting up EES? It stands for Extreme Excursion Scheme. He said he dreamed up the idea at his secondary school, when he was twelve. It came to him while he was waiting for rugby practice to start. Like a fun run. The entrants had to do a five mile jog... pushing a wheelbarrow full of manure. Cost two pounds to enter plus a cigarette. First prize was twenty pounds and a wicked reputation.

He gave the proceeds to the school garden – organic fertilizer – brill hey? There were six hundred boarders at his school.

'Choice, always offer a choice, Tilly. Draws them in. Get them to choose what you've got to offer,' FJ told me.

'The kids at his school could choose – another look at his old porn magazines or a chance to win money. It was a no brainer.

'He had a bit of problem at the start with the Headmaster – so not convinced. FJ's father got summoned to the school to discuss FJ's behaviour. FJ argued that the task was happy chappies keeping fit and doing good for the community.

'Even the police supported him 'cause they got their horse shit moved for free. I'm not sure manure would work for me at my school but Jane and me can see the idea's got scope. FJ also made some serious income by selling the fags on the side to the kids who didn't run. Business went from there really, he said.'

'Very entrepreneurial, as you say Tilly,' Psycho nodded.

'Yes and EES was his brainchild. He got to travel legally and on his own, away from his rents. FJ's tried joyriding, gambling, skateboarding and all sorts of extreme sports. Anything that involved speed.

'Bacchanalian, FJ calls it, Booze, burgers, bullshit and babes whenever he wants.

'Jane and me think the last one's wishful thinking, mostly. From what we could see, he was pretty shy when it came to real girls. Like he blushed when he talked to Shazza. We think he'd need lots of alcohol and drugs, when he hits the clubs, to make it with girls.'

'Perhaps his time with you Tilly has made a significant contribution to his understanding of the modern female?'

'You might be right. I gave him some tips on how us younger women might have a bit of problem with him.'

'Really, how did you do that?'

'I said it would be better if FJ stood for flak-jacket? Frederick is a bit of a nonce name.

'He told me that was not a nice word for a young girl to know.

'Jane and me know lots of nonces,' I said, and when he raised his eyebrows I introduced him to Jane. He was okay with Jane, even shook her hand, like Yousef. Quite sweet really, seeing he's a grown-up boy.

' "I think you've got the word mixed up," he said.

' "No, sex offenders, rule forty-five of British prisons and segregation, that's nonce. The Oxford English Dictionary suggests its etymology is linked to the Victorian term, nancy boy, referring to homosexual males..."

' "Okay Tilly," FJ said, "I can see you've done your homework. Your school is certainly different to where I went."

' "Internet research," I told him. "Me and Jane are the class experts on sexual deviation. FJ, if you want to know the chat line website where you can talk to real live nonces, it's... "

‘ "Thanks but no thanks, Tilly. I like my women older than sixteen. And you need to be careful. There are some really bad people out there. How do you know they're telling the truth? Just because they say something on the Internet..."

'Of course those nonces are liars. Jane and me know that. We just like having a laugh. I told him Jane's been propositioned by nearly fifteen sexual deviants in one month.

'He said he didn't want to know. Sexual deviation is outside EES.

'I gave him another tip – could be a new market. Adrenalin is the common link. If his customers wanted to get pumping with something scary then maybe doing it with whips and dildos could add an extra erotic thrill!'

'What did he say to that idea?' asked Psycho. I could see she was quite impressed with my line of thinking.

‘ "Too much information! Let's change the topic. But if we ever get out of here alive Tilly, I promise to change the name of my company to Flak Jacket Tours."

‘ "You mean when, don't you?" I said. "Yousef is a big softy. He won't hurt us. He just wants people to listen to what he has to say."

‘ "Don't we all?" FJ sighed.

'His father didn't want to listen when he told him about his big idea for the tour operator business.

‘ "Just like my SWMBO," I told him.

‘ "I'm planning trips for people who wanted to test their physical limits and push their imaginations."

‘ "Foolhardy," FJ's father replied. "No one will risk backing your business."

‘ "Wrong dad, a local tour operator already has."

164

'You see it all worked 'cause FJ went to see a tour operator who already had the contacts, licenses and insurance. FJ put some packages together. Helli-sking down glaciers, white-water rafting on bamboo platforms, wind surfing safaris, camping in a cave full of bats and spiders.

'Jane reckons we should send that Giselle on a spiders' trip and leave her in the cave.

'The tour operator loved his ideas and gave him his perfect job. FJ got to dream, travel and earn. He even persuaded a sportswear company to sponsor an extreme travel kit. They made heaps when their clients bought it. The tour operations kept getting bigger and bigger, great profits. After three years FJ had his own brochure, with his face on the cover… and a sports car.

' "I've already got a reputation in the industry for adventure holidays with a difference. I'm going to make it Tilly, big time," he told me.

Way to go, me and Jane want to have a Maserati before I'm twenty five.'

'FJ and Dr L must have had something in common,' said Psycho.

'Yes they did talk about making money out of tourists.'

FJ said, 'Go on, Grandad. Bit of a mover and shaker in your time were you?'

'I do numbers,' said Dr L. 'How many under twenty five year olds can you stuff into a bar with bad taste entertainment? I'll leave my sociology colleagues to work out why they choose to spend their money doing it.'

'You're missing out on the fun if you spend all your time on the data,' replied FJ.

'Fun… this place? These people are the pits. Why don't you and I go find somewhere quiet? I'd really appreciate the opportunity to talk about your tour operations.'

165

'Somewhere quiet at a party for tourists with free booze? You're a laugh Livingstone – for a political economist that is,' FJ told him.

'So why was FJ at the Garden of Eden party?' asked Psycho.

'It was a whole new project for FJ. He wanted to sell really cool experiences like swimming with sharks. That's why he came to the resort. Feasibility visit, he called it.

'Jane and me agreed we could do fees-and-ability too. If we were going to be entrepreneurs, we'd start with a visit to every Disneyland on the planet.

'FJ'd done his homework. He knew there were sharks where we were.'

'What was FJ planning to do with sharks?' Psycho asked.

'Sharks weren't a problem, he said. Making sure the tourists could see sharks but not get eaten by them – well that was his challenge.

' "Word of mouth, Tilly, with all limbs and life intact, is a prerequisite to successful bookings."

'I didn't quite get that, but it sounded great. Jane and me wanted to know how he was going to do it. FJ said he'd found a local family that made large crates for exporting live fish.

' "If those crates could stay in the water keeping the fish alive and the predators out, then why not humans, instead of fins, inside them?"

'Even better, FJ discovered that this family had a relative whose son spoke excellent English. Guess who? You won't believe it!'

'Yousef?' Psycho guessed.

'Yes, Yousef, 'cause he'd been studying at a British university.'

'I just know Yousef and I are going to hit it off big time,' FJ told his father.' It'll be a blast.'

'It's quite funny when you think about it, isn't it? Blast – Jane and me thought it'd make a good joke. Jane says it'd be a big bang sort of punch line.'

'Do you think Yousef and FJ would've laughed?' asked Psycho.

Jane nudged me. Signal to shut up.

29. Yousef

I am Yousef. I speak on behalf of a local group. We call ourselves *My Land, My Way*. We raise the issue of tourism. The details of the debate on sustainable tourism are not what I wish to present today. But the principles are important and our demands reflect these.

We say there are three principles to be addressed. They are not negotiable. They must be acknowledged and respected.

First, this is our land.

Second, we must have a say in what happens to our land.

Third, we all should benefit from use of the land, today and tomorrow.

Therefore *My Land, My Way* insists that a legally constituted organisation is established. This must be internationally recognised so that all parties can have a voice in how our land is developed, how the benefits are distributed, and how negative economic, cultural, social, environmental and political impacts can be reduced.

We suggest that *My Land, My Way* is a temporary structure to ensure these outcomes in accordance with our principles.

We apologise if our strategy has caused inconvenience. Our intention is not, and never has been, to harm any individual, foreign or local, in our aims.

However, we feel we have been forced to pursue this path in order to gain access to the media.

The world needs to hear our entreaty for a fairer way to secure justice and transparency.

Your voice, our voice, my land, your holiday, my way, your way – like the winds, things can change.

30. Jane

Tilly has added three more portraits to her portfolio. Ma little friend is now mix and matching her Basquiat influences with her naive. Y'all have to admire that dexterity. It takes a real genius to distil the essence of greatness and mould it to your own. Not that Ah agree with everything Tilly thinks. Ah don't rate that Shazza. Ah agree with SWMBO. She told Tilly's dad that Shazza had no class. Ma Tilly needs to grow into her own style. Ah am sure as a dodo is dead that a bleached pineapple hairdo and a dolphin tattoo is not a signature look for ma best friend and role model.

But that Shazza sure is a laugh. Except that Ah think some people laugh AT her not WITH her. That's not kind.

Me and Tilly busted a gut over Dr L. He looks like he has been cooked. Never mind the cannibals grabbing him. What a dufus. Even his mum avoids him. When Tilly did the Romans we spent ages on the Internet. Classical civilisations – who knew life was so exciting in the olden days? Those Spartans, who were sort of Greek, used to chuck kids they didn't want over a cliff. Not all the sites agreed that was true but me and Tilly thought the idea had merit. Especially as the kids they killed were nearly always boys. Just imagine how many bullies you could get rid of? That Jeremy for one. Maybe Dr L's mum would have been glad to see her brat go for a walk off the cliff.

Ma Tilly was scared that the Spartans would chuck her off a cliff.

'Did they have kids like me?' she wanted to know.

No info about this on the Internet so we gave up. Maybe ma Tilly's condition is one of those modern things like how plastic can give you cancer 'cause it makes your cells going wonky.

The drawing of FJ is okay. Anybody who wants to swim with sharks is bonkers. But we forgave him. A grown-up who talks nicely to me and Yousef is pretty well adjusted.

Shazza

The girl with EVERYTHING

Dr Livingstone

He is a hairy and boring doctor.

FJ

He is not scared of sharks.

Not that Tilly and me could work out who was bonkers and who was bad from the blog. There's a lot of political nutters out there in cyberland. Bad Apple is still tracking us. Tilly scores him big time. I'm not convinced. He might just be one big perv!

 JANE DOLL: blog bits and bobs

Attitude
Think that you can, then you will
Think that you can't then you won't

Jane needs to do it with you

Blow up
In the Garden of Eden
I was there
It was so*ooo* unfair
Please help me
GET EVEN
What they say on the news
is not true
SIGN UP
To my internet campaign
Justice is the aim
Jane needs to do it with you
WANT TO DO IT with JANE DOLL?
Great plan, lots of fun, internet savvies
required.

Vive the new world order!!!

Re: Jane needs to do it with you
<<<By Randy Renegade >>>

Luv the idea Jane Doll. The end will justify
the means. Bring on the revolution. What
skills do you need?

Re: Jane needs to do it with you
<<<By Bad Apple >>>

Jane Doll – willing, waiting and wanting.
Blow jobs, bondage – what a plan, count
me in.

Re: Jane needs to do it with you
<<<By No Regrets >>>

Our group will help. Let cyberspace battle
begin. Down with multinational media pigs.
Up democracy and people power. Go Jane, go.

Re: Jane needs to do it with you
<<<By Watch your back >>>

Beware the big boys Jane. They will fight
back. God may be on your side but He
don't own the banks.

31. Tilly

Psycho asked me about our release from the Conservatory Bar.

I felt Jane stiffen. Bad memories flooding into her bullet holed head. I squeezed her hand. She relaxed but kept her hand in mine.

'I've got to talk to walk, right?' I replied to Psycho.

'If you're asking me do you have to tell me about it, then no,' she said. 'It's not an order. It would help me, of course, to write a more comprehensive report. Then we might be able to help with your sleeplessness.'

'I told you. I can sleep... just not at the moment. Soon I will, once Jane's got her stuff together.'

'I understand your concern for Jane. She's very lucky. Not everyone looks after their doll so well. But Tilly, I do need to focus on you and what you need to do to stay healthy. Jane is Jane but you are my patient. Therefore I have to put your needs first. After all if you get sick from being too tired, then who is going to look after Jane?'

'This doesn't come under Tuckman, does it?' I said.

'No, this is about one person, you, Matilda Henderson-Smythe. It's not about group dynamics. It's about helping you to sleep at night and stay awake during the day. Your parents tell me you were a good sleeper before... Yousef. I'd like to be able to help you become that good sleeper again. If I could understand what happened with Yousef, then maybe we can work out what to do next.'

'Will I have to keep coming to see you?'

'Not unless you want to.'

'Jane and me wouldn't mind, you know. But we wouldn't want to keep talking about this holiday stuff. I could teach you how to play chess if you want. You could pay me in chocolates.'

'Now that's a thought. I suspect I'd need to buy in a lot of chocolates if I was ever going to beat you at chess,' smiled Psycho. 'Was Yousef a good chess player?'

'Nah, life is too short for games, he said. But Jane and me think Yousef would have been ace 'cause he thinks a lot before he does things. And he said he was an engineer. That means he could think in sequences. That's what chess is all about.'

'It might have been interesting to see who would have won in a play off between you, Yousef and Giselle.'

'No contest – me!'

'You seem very sure.'

'I am. Yousef's a softie. He'd let me win, even if I wasn't really the best, 'cause I'm a girl and younger than him.'

'That's rather a nice characteristic, isn't it?' Psycho asked.

'Yes, but it's so not a good attitude if you want to win a championship. No point in being polite. You've got to focus on the pieces on the chessboard, not the people sitting there. Fatal if you lose your concentration. Jane doesn't say a thing when I'm playing, no matter what.'

'And you're sure you'd beat Giselle?'

'Too easy! She'd be relaxed to start, 'cause she'd think I was just special needs playing kid level chess. And once she wised up I was serious it'd be too late. Anyway, I'd have a plan B. Now that I know her weakness.'

'Oh, and what plan might that be?'

'I'd have Jane next to me. Jane would have a big spider under her dress, pinned on her knickers. Diversion to annihilation in one move.'

'Tilly, are spiders allowed into chess competitions?'

'Oh, it wouldn't be a real one. Just a real looking, plastic one. One of those big, black, hairy looking tarantulas. Not poisonous, even it was real.'

175

'Seems a questionable way to make sure you win.'

'I took your advice and looked up Machiavelli.'

'Did you now?'

'Jane thought it was a bit boring. I didn't get it, not really. Too much talk, not enough action. Idea was brill but I don't think it'll be a best seller for the kids I know. We spent the whole night on the Internet chatting about how the end justifies the means. It solved everything.'

'Lots of people would argue that Machiavelli is not the best principle,' said Psycho.

'Well Jane says there are laws that are just laws. But they're not real justice.'

'What do you think Yousef would say?'

'That freedom of speech is fair enough. That what people say is the truth, sometimes isn't. That Giselle was an arsehole on truth issues.'

'That sounds like you're very angry with Giselle.'

'Jane says I should have told the whole story. Then the viewers could make up their own minds. Like when something kicks off at school. The teachers ask everyone to tell their bit. If it's Mrs Watson then you know you're going to get a fair hearing. She's the best judge. Even Jeremy agrees.'

'What does Mrs Watson do after she's heard all of you telling your own side of the story?'

'She makes a decision. She always gets it right about who did the bad stuff. Then she makes them do something to try and make it right. And they have to apologise in front of us all. That usually works too. Not always with Jeremy though. ''Cause he can be sneaky, just like that Giselle, and do something horrible later. Like when Mrs Watson's not around. Or after school when there's no grown-ups. Jeremy is just one big turd. He knows he can get away with it.'

'Mrs Watson sounds like a good teacher. She practises

what we call restorative justice. It's when you have people who have done the hurtful things talk to the people they have hurt.'

'Exactly, that's what Jane said. Remember, when I made Jeremy pay for my photograph. When he was being a bully?'

'Hmm, that's one interpretation, Tilly. Taking responsibility for your actions helps you to understand their impact on other people.'

'You mean you get to know how other people feel about what you've done?'

'Exactly, Tilly.'

'Then you should get that Giselle in here and talk to her about this stuff. She so needs therapy.'

'I'm not following your thoughts very easily. Can you explain that for me please?'

'You need to look at the interviews she did. Like the ones at the airport, when we were coming back to England, after it was all over. Then I can explain if you don't get it. But you will.'

Psycho loaded the disc into her DVD player and fast forwarded it to the place in the interview I had described. Jane patted by arm. Well done, my friend is what that pat meant.

Giselle spoke directly to camera.

'Let's hear what one of the hostages, Dr Livingstone, a world expert on tourism development has to say on his ordeal.

'You're about to fly home, Doctor, lucky to be alive. Can you tell us what you've learnt from your experience?'

'We call them hotspots in the business. Blights on global development. Travel and tourism is one of the

177

largest global industries. It represents ten point seven percent of the total value of world trade and generates eight point two percent of total global employment. It's a key sector within the sustainability debate.'

'Ah, that's very interesting I'm sure Doctor, but our viewers really want to know how you coped under such pressure. You were there, in the Conservatory Bar, held at gunpoint. Did you think the terrorists were going to kill you?'

'I thought you wanted a serious response. I'm involved in critical academic research here. This experience will validate my funding and the World Tourism Organisation will be publishing my report. The variables included events beyond my control. After all, nobody can buy insurance against terrorism.'

'Thank you. We're out of time. I'm going to talk to some of the other hostages, while the world wonders if it's safe to travel.'

32. Jack

'Talking is a cheap option.'

That's what Colonel Rupert tells us.

'If the terrorists say they are willing to negotiate we could get a positive outcome with no casualties. I've spoken to Whitehall. No update on intelligence about Yousef and his friends. Permission granted to take control as soon as. Priority is to get the hostages released alive.'

Me mate, Corporal Cecil, grins and whispers when the Colonel turns his back, 'Kids' party time. Walk in and take the sweeties out.'

'Speed in theatre will be critical as we've got international media arriving en masse. So I'm told. Discretion is a key factor for MOD Press Office,' the Colonel advises.

'No change there!' spits Cecil. 'What are those buggers thinking? No reliable info but still they expect us to achieve, achieve, achieve.'

'I've requested a media blackout until after resolution of the situation. Reply from Whitehall is request not feasible,' concludes the Colonel.

I want to tell him that it's okay. I've got a friendly Brit journalist on side. Cecil second guesses me.

'Don't go there. Press is press. Can't trust any of them. If Rupert finds out you're on course to shagging one of them, matey you're up there with our targets,' he warns.

I blush. In my dreams... but she'd never consider me that way. Would she?

I say to Cecil, 'Giselle's not like that. She's a student journo – just got lucky being in the right place at the right time.'

'She saw you coming. I tell you, press is press whether they're BBC or some young blonde out to prove she's worth the job! As soon as she's got her headline she won't remember your name.'

179

I don't tell him we've exchanged contact details for our first date in London. Gran will be well impressed.

33. Tilly

'That's not really what happened, you know,' I told Psycho when the interview finished on the DVD. 'Giselle and Dr L had a big argument. That was *sooo* much more interesting that what you just saw on the TV.'

'Why do you say that?' Psycho asked.

'Well after he said that stuff, Giselle told her cameraman to stop filming and snapped at the Doc, "News is all about use it or lose it."

'Dr L didn't get it so she said, "You're boring! Liven it up. Viewers don't want statistics. They want human interest, passion, drama, laughter, tears. Tell me how the hostage experience has impacted on you personally. Reaction not research – okay to start again?"

' "No," said the Doc, "I'm not doing this. It's just proves what's wrong with the Garden of Eden, the original and this constructed namesake. God should have kept Eve out of the original apple orchard so Adam could get on with his work."

' "Oh no, not this again," Giselle groaned.

' "It's all became a gendered tussle," Dr L shouted, "instead of reasoned debate on land rights and appropriate development, you want the opinion of a mob of tourists, including a fat kid with Down Syndrome. And you, one of my best students, calling yourself the media. My students pride themselves on being the voice of reason."

' "Listen, this is the real world. I have to listen to you droning on in lectures. In front of the camera I'm in charge. Get it?"

' "Who listens to a screaming blonde?" Dr L sneered. "I tell you it was just like Adam. Yousef got subverted. Calling him a bone fide terrorist is a joke."

'Jane and me were really, really mad that he called me

181

fat. Dr L's a fatty too but I wouldn't be so rude to call him that when other people could hear.'

Psycho nodded so I guess she agreed with me.

'Do you know what that Giselle did then?' I asked Psycho.

She shook her head.

'Giselle said, "Perk it up or piss off mate. I've got ratings to keep up."'

'Jane said we should file the perk and piss saying in our folder for further use. I plan to use it on Jeremy. I think television viewers would love to see the whole argument between Dr L and Giselle. Better than hearing all that boring stuff, don't you think?'

'You are probably right, Tilly,' said Psycho. 'Perhaps the channel thought it might sound too much like a reality show, if they included the argument. News is supposed to more about the facts, I think.'

'Who makes the decision about what facts and interviews to have in the programme and what to leave out?'

'I don't know, Tilly – the editor? Whoever is the boss of the programme, I guess.'

'You heard of Goebbels?' I asked her.

'The Nazi?'

'Yes, he was famous 'cause he controlled all the media in Germany. People only got to hear and read what he said they could. Just like Giselle really?'

'That's not quite correct, Tilly. Giselle isn't in charge of everything to do with her broadcast. She collected all the interviews with the people at the Garden of Eden Hotel and maybe she suggested what bits should be included in the programme but... well it's different to what happens in totalitarian states.'

'It's still censorship, whatever they try and say. Yousef didn't get to say what he wanted to. We did.'

'I need to think about what you've said. Perhaps we can discuss it later?'

'Rent speak again! That's what SWMBO says when she wants to change the subject.'

34. Giselle

I love speaking direct to camera. I can imagine people all over the world listening to my every word. It's such a buzz. No wonder media's got a name for power. I'm up for that. Power to my voice. Power to me. I lean towards the camera as I speak to give a sense of intimacy. I'm telling you... and you... and you... something very special.

'The climate at the Garden of Eden Hotel is changing as I broadcast live. Instead of bikinis and straw hats that you would expect to see around these parts, it's balaclavas and battle gear. Is it all about to turn ugly?

'In the last twenty minutes two more signs have appeared on the glass door... same handwriting as before. Still no clue on who wrote the words but speculation is that the script looks like something a child might do. For security reasons, we've been asked not to televise the signs.

'But, in the public interest, I decide to reveal the messages.'

I signal Nigel to keep the camera rolling. He zooms in on the signs.

The first states OUR HOME V YOUR HOLIDAY!

The second asks, TIME TO TALK?

'Who is it that wants to talk? And what do they want to talk about?'

After I finish the live update I see Jack, the soldier boy, gazing at me. I also see his sour faced boss glaring.

Up you for a chocolate frog, Colonel Rupert!

I wave at Jack. He blushes. The Colonel turns to see who is my target for flirting with. Jack looks at the ground. I'm not sure whether he's escaped the Colonel's eye or not. I don't risk anything more. Jack could be very important to me. Probably not in the way he is hoping.

35. Yousef

I sent a written message to the hotel management. They promised to hand it to the authorities. The message reads:

My Land, My Way, our group, want people to hear what we have to say.

To hear our message the world must know *My Land, My Way* exists.

To achieve our objective we have invited one representative from the international press, camped outside the Garden of Eden Hotel, to come to the glass doors of the Conservatory Bar.

I, Yousef, will meet with that person to discuss broadcasting our demands.

I acknowledge that this strategy is not ideal. But it is expedient. It is the only option available to us. If we did not have thirty foreign guests I know that the world media would not be here and would therefore, be unaware of our message.

My Land, My Way demands are:

The opportunity to read our statement to camera, unedited.

A signed agreement that a forum on sustainable tourism development will be held at this resort, within six months. At this forum, all voices including *My Land, My Way* and its perspectives on tourism development, will be represented and heard.

When the broadcast is complete *My Land, My Way* will release immediately all the detained guests who have been kept safe and well cared for.

Insha'Allah.

36. Giselle

Holy, moley, big one or what? Opportunity of the year – me, I'm going into the bunker, so to speak. The terrorists want to talk to someone in the press.

Result – I'm going in alone to talk to Yousef.

Boy wonder in a dishdash and me, EXCLUSIVE.

One up on Colonel Rupert pooper-trooper. Wants to spoil my sunshine. Shove it man in uniform, it's my way to scoop of the week.

I can already feel that applause. BAFTA documentary winner, here I come.

Do I wear something on my head? Look like I get the whole Muslim thingy. No, won't look great in the broadcast.

I check my shirt. Still bearing up fine. It'll be easy for the cameraman to get his white balance right if I stay this way. Bit of lip gloss won't go amiss though.

I hang my head towards the ground to ruffle the curls, straighten up, apply the gloss, brief Nigel.

I look around at the troops positioned in the bushes, ready for action, covering my back as I head towards the Conservatory Bar where the hostages are waiting. I'm pretty sure I see Jack amongst them. I don't wave. He and me need to focus.

Battle stations, here I come... minus the fireworks.

37. Jack

The fireworks were scheduled only as back up. If the operation went pear shaped. It should have been text book. It was clear that the so-called terrorists were inexperienced youths. We knew they were armed. With what and how competent were unknowns. All signs were that the hostages were alive and not in immediate danger.

Colonel Rupert believed that Yousef and his supporters were most likely talkers and not fighters.

'No reported history of radicalisation or military training. Green light to peaceful negotiation. Usual policy of no ransom applies,' he instructed.

The Colonel was well brassed off that Giselle got involved.

'I told that blonde pundit to keep away. The bitch refused to listen. Claimed it was in the public interest.'

Afterwards, when we were all trying to work out what to do in the mess, I tried to help when I suggested to him that maybe Giselle was as much a victim as Yousef.

'Bullshit,' he swore, 'she was always out to play Lady Courage.'

38. Giselle

It took courage I can tell you.

Standing there, in the dark, those pesky cicadas screaming abuse. I reapplied the citronella when I got the chance. You can't be too careful in this part of the world. Creepy crawlies lurk everywhere.

'Bloody thorns,' Nigel, the cameraman, whispered, 'I hope they're not poisonous.'

'Get a grip,' I snapped, 'this is going to be the scoop of the month. You getting crucified in concrete paradise is not on my radar.'

'Love you too,' he replied.

That's one of Nigel's good points. He doesn't get rattled easily. Always goes with the flow. He drives me nuts at university sometimes – rather clingy – wants to be part of the special group. That's what we blondes get called when we hang out at the student bar on Friday evenings. All drinks for one pound during the first thirty minutes of happy hour. Those of us in the special group never buy our own. That's what makes us so special. Treat us nicely and you might wangle an invitation to buy us another at full price. Student boys – all rather predictable!

'Shut it,' the Colonel ordered. Nigel went silent. I rather fancied Colonel Rupert at that moment. There's something about an older, no nonsense man in uniform that brings out the fluff in me. I couldn't wait for the debrief after the whole caboodle was finished. I wanted a final comment set against Yousef being taken away in chains… at gun point… by my admiring soldier, Jack the lad.

From experience, I know blondes always have an advantage.

39. Jack

At cadet training, they teach you that the advantage, in any hostile situation, is to take your opponent by surprise.

If you're quick you can win with minimum casualties and little loss of face.

If not, the consequences can be dire.

40. Giselle

Dire circumstances demand direct action. What would you have done if you had been me?

I turned to camera and began.

'I'm Giselle and this is your sixty second update, live from the hostage situation. In a few minutes I'll be walking up to those glass doors you can see on your screen. There I'll be talking to Yousef, head of the terrorist gang who call themselves My Land, My Way.

'I'm the only journalist that the terrorists are prepared to talk to.

'What will they want? Is this the break through we've all been waiting for?'

It might make sense with hindsight. But it's not a little thing you know. Loads of people suffer. All ages, men and women, every group is represented. Phobias are a recognised behavioural disorder with well documented publications. Whole departments devoted. Prestigious funding supports serious research. Just ask Heinrich Heine University in Dusseldorf, Feinberg School of Medicine in Chicago or Social Sciences at Nottingham Trent. That's where some of the world gurus on arachnophobia hang out. They'll tell you the facts. I've contacted them all.

I was a victim. There wasn't anything I could do in the circumstances.

41. Jack

'Anything that friggin' cow wouldn't do for a story?'

That's what Colonel Rupert said about Giselle when it kicked off.

'A real fuck up!'

Corporal Cecil's remark would have upset my Gran. She doesn't like men swearing. But Cecil was right. I wanted to go see Giselle and tell her it was going to be okay.

But I didn't.

Because it wasn't going to be alright.

For a lot of people it was a grade A, one hundred per cent stuff up.

The Colonel was adamant. 'The media is going to have to take responsibility this time. Sort it out Whitehall. My troops did well. They were here. The rest of the world was not. Blame culture is not in my brief.'

42. Giselle

Don't blame me. It could have happened to anyone.

I was in front of the camera, broadcasting direct to the world.

And then... I gulped... it felt like a tickle. Something was moving up the leg of my trousers. Legs, lots of them, marching upward, ankle to shin. I remember thinking what if. What if it kept climbing to my knee, to my thigh, to my...? All I could focus on was that my socks and citronella came from London. But this tickle was local. A tarantula? Poison? I could die.

That's why I screamed when I did... and kept screaming. You don't get much time when a venomous spider bites. I knew I was a goner.

'Stop the camera, I'm dead,' I hollered.

Nigel, the cameraman, replied that he already had stopped rolling.

'Cut the language and get a grip,' he said. 'Your mascara's running down your gob.'

It wasn't my fault.

Yousef could have moved out of the way. He was holding a stupid doll. What sort of terrorist wants to hold a press conference with a doll in his hand?

The troops should have seen the doll was not a gun. I mean have you ever seen a gun with a blonde curly hammer? I asked Jack that very question afterwards. He just shrugged.

I finished my live broadcast.

'We're live again from the centre of the action,' I said. 'It's the go code. We have movement on all fronts. All I can say is it's chaos here on the ground.

'The troops have gone in firing with everything

193

they've got. The terrorists' so-called safe place has been tear-gassed and bombed. Our good guys are fighting back for freedom.'

Afterwards Colonel Rupert didn't register any emotion. He scared me.

I wanted to tell him that sometimes things go wrong. The press don't create the mess. We just report it.

The Colonel didn't strike me as empathetic.

I left him with the remains.

Nigel scampered too.

Jack stayed with his boss. The army look after their own.

43. Jack

My mate, Corporal Cecil, heard that Whitehall ordered a report on the process and outcomes of the army invasion of the Garden of Eden Hotel.

Colonel Rupert was livid and told us all, 'You can't trust the news to tell you the truth.'

I told him that fat kid, Tilly Henderson-Smythe, summed it up perfectly. I overheard her telling the Reverend Angus, 'That boss man in the army sure gave Giselle the look. Worse than my mother's death ray one. Jane and me totally got why.'

I didn't realise at that stage Jane was her doll. After forty hours it was touching to see a teenager like her respond so tenderly to a toy with a bullet scar.

The Colonel smiled but said nothing. I guess he knew I had a soft spot for Giselle. That's the problem when you can see both sides of the mess. Gran wouldn't find it hard. She'd be right sure who the best tea cup would be reserved for. Gran isn't big on the sisterhood.

44. Giselle

It didn't matter that nobody would talk to me.

Jack did check to see if he could find any signs of a spider bite. He couldn't. Nigel was embarrassed to be anywhere near me. He probably thought I made it up. Jack said he believed that I believed it was a poisonous spider.

'One hundred percent,' he said. 'I believe you're a good person Giselle. And just because you're beautiful and clever doesn't mean you can't be scared of things – like spiders.'

I wasn't going to do purdah for being human. If the army wanted professional, then that's what I was going to be. I ordered Nigel to set up the camera and crossed live to London with the latest update. I stood beside Colonel Rupert who was so surprised he didn't dare move away.

'After forty hours of tense waiting and negotiations, all's quiet in the Garden of Eden. The siege is over. The terrorists are no longer a threat. And as we wait for the first of the hostages to emerge, I'm joined by Colonel Rupert Higgs-White, the British commander who lead the daring rescue mission.

'Colonel, you must be pleased that it's gone so well?'

'Our goal was achieved with minimum losses.'

'Can you tell us, in your own words, what happened?'

'I am unable to discuss the operation at this stage other than to say all hostages are accounted for and safe. No British military personnel have been wounded or killed. Details of the offensive will be released later today by the Ministry of Defence. I have no further comment to make.'

I went for the jugular and smiled as I asked, '*Colonel, do you think the outcome justified the approach?*'

'*I don't focus on the morality of the situation, only results. I expect the media can empathize with that?*'

'*That sounds rather profound and something for our viewers to consider.*'

I signalled to Nigel to stop recording. Both he and the Colonel walked away.

The worst thing about being lied to is knowing you're not worth the truth.

45. Jack

The truth is that soldiers know that they succeed or fail because they do things together. In the army you are stronger as a group than you are alone.

Colonel Rupert tells me that, in his experience, journalists succeed at someone else's expense. Big egos don't make for good friends. He believes the ethos of hacks in the field is – get there first, get the story, bugger anyone else. It's me, me, me, first, second and third.

Death and respect are so final.

I still fancy Giselle but I know we're not going to meet up in London once this all over. I guess I always knew that. But it was nice to pretend.

I thought I might buy her a present. She could do with a course in how to beat her fear of spiders. Otherwise she's going to be a complete dud as a journalist, especially if she's travelling to weird and wonderful parts of the world. If she can't cope with spiders, she'll melt down with snakes and scorpions.

46. Giselle

My final broadcast was to be from the airport where the hostage survivors would be ready and waiting to board their flight back to London. It's not the sort of news you put on a postcard. It was worth my while to get an overview. My editor in London adored the idea.

'A fit finale,' he said. 'Look forward to getting the footage.'

I love re-playing it – made my name. I've had two offers for a job as soon as I've graduated... decisions, decisions.

'What about me?' asked Nigel. 'We were a team Giselle.'

In your dreams Nigel. People using a camera are easy to find. It takes real talent to find the subject and nail an interview.

Mind you that wretched Jane Doll site needs investigating. I've got a bad feeling about who that might be. How difficult it will be to bring down a retard is not making me lose any sleep. She might have caused me some grief but as my editor said, 'Being cast as the villain still buys you an international reputation. Blog sites are ten minute wonders... unless you're a celebrity.'

If I'm right, and I usually am, a retard teenage dumpling will be piddle easy to silence. I've learnt a thing or seven about how to troll effectively.

To remind myself just how good I am, I loaded the interview into my DVD machine and pressed the play button. Those blonde curls of mine were the highlight of that airport departure area.

'For the thirty brave survivors it's definitely been the holiday of a lifetime,' I said, smiling to camera.

'Behind me, you can see that it's almost a carnival atmosphere in the departure lounge. People are mingling. Strangers before they arrived, these intrepid

tourists have become friends forever. On the surface there's little evidence of the extreme danger these passengers were subjected to by a gang of local terrorists.

'I'm joined by the Reverend Angus, a British subject, who has been living at the Garden of Eden Hotel. He works with guests and the local community during the holiday season.

'Reverend, how have you coped with the situation?'

'God has shown His mercy. All of us are unharmed.'

'Weren't you frightened what these Islamic terrorists would do to you?'

'Yousef was a Muslim. I don't regard him as a terrorist. He wanted his opinion to be heard. I believe he should have been allowed to speak to the press. I don't agree with how he went about arranging that. Seizing tourists is not a good plan. But at no time did I feel that any of us were in any danger from Yousef and his group of campaigners.'

'Some might say that's a very Christian attitude, Reverend. But it's not proved to be the most appropriate way to resolve cultural differences or debate about development,' I continued.

'I try to remember that there is good in everyone, whatever their faith. It's our duty to look for the best. God and Allah would agree on that.'

I signalled to Nigel to collect some cutaways while I repositioned to interview the others.

'My next guests are tour operator, FJ, and resort representative Wayne. In the wake of the siege, gentlemen, how optimistic are you both feeling about this place as a tourist destination?'

'It's still a great place to holiday,' said Wayne. 'It's the first time there's been an incident like this. You can see it was dealt with very quickly. None of our guests were injured. Our company has ensured that all our clients have been upgraded so that they'll fly home in style.'

'It's a hiccup. The resort won an international tourism award in its first year of operation. FJ Tours will be carrying out a full health and security check but I'm sure this incident is a one off. Nothing but a few youngsters on the rampage. Problem solved, business as usual.' FJ smiled.

'There were guns. Tourists were held hostage. People died,' I replied.

'People who disregard the law have to accept the consequences. The tourists were not in any real danger. The guns weren't even real, it turned out. No foreigners were hurt. Law and order were restored very quickly. Let's not sensationalise what really happened. A group of locals, who disagreed with their own elected government, chose the wrong way to get their views heard. The local community didn't support this action. They're behind tourism development. It's brought jobs and helped create a prosperous future for what was a very poor area. FJ Tours will be back here next season. We're planning a swim with the sharks experience – exciting stuff.'

I turned to the holiday rep and asked, 'What about you Wayne? Will you want to come back to a place where your life was threatened?'

'I'm a professional nomad, Giselle. Where the company wants me to work, I go. Next stop is a ski resort in Switzerland. Who knows after that? But I'd be very content to work here again. The water's *warm, the sand's clean, the sunshine guaranteed and the lobster is to dream about.'*

I signalled again to Nigel. These comments were sounding like advertisements. We moved. Time to find some humour and lift the broadcast.

'No doubt the development debate between whose holiday, whose home will continue in the weeks ahead. As the five terrorists shot dead are buried and the tourists return with their own stories, I've asked some of our brave travellers to share their comments on the experience.

'Just what memories will they be taking home?
The camera panned the group.

'Hi boys, do you want to show us what your souvenirs are? Just hold them up for the camera. What is that?'

'Shrapnel – from the shoot-out. Taking it home for me mum,' said Tom.

'Yeah and I got this hat, man,' interjected Rick. *'Right off one of them dead terrorists. You can see the hole where the bullet went through.'*

'It's called a keffiyeh – traditional Arab head dress. It's often worn with the long white tunic called a disdasha,' I explained. I'm sure lots of my viewers will want full knowledge and the correct terms.

'Yeah, whatever,' replied Rick. *'Where I come from real blokes wear jeans, not a white dress.'*

'You might have a spot of bother boys with the shrapnel. I'm not sure security will let you take it on board.'

'Why not? I earned it.'

'He's my hero,' said Shazza flaunting a diamante

202

earring and revealing the dolphin tattoo on her left breast.

'Get a life, Shazza' said Tom. *'Who cacked himself when those nutters took us prisoner?'*

'We was all scared,' replied Tom.

'I wasn't,' said Shazza. *'Rick held my hand and I knew we was okay.'*

'Make me puke, why don't you?'

'Wanna make me?'

'Come on Shaz, stop it Tom, we don't want a fight. Not after all the shit we've been through,' said Rick.

'He's got to apologise first,' said Sharon.

'In your dreams. Fuck off you slag,' Tom replied.

'Hey, who you calling a slag? And cut the swearing. We're on the telly.'

Perfect – a script writer couldn't have done it better. My editor was going to love it. Reality television, sky rocket ratings. Time to move on to our little heroine, Tilly Henderson-Smythe and her family.

'What have you got to say, Tilly?

'What's fuck off you slag mean?'

'Language, Tilly, language, we're on television!' corrected Mrs Henderson-Smythe.

'Nothing dumpling,' replied Mr Henderson-Smythe. *'It's just what friends say to each other at the airport. It's a sort of good-bye saying.'*

'Like au revoir?'

'Along those lines, dumpling.'

'I would just like to say,' began Tilly's mother to camera, *'I don't intend to set foot outside Britain again. What an experience! If it wasn't the locals trying to kill us...'*

'*The hotel made us feel very special,*' finished Tilly's father.

'*The kids' club sucked,*' added Tilly.

'*Tilly!*' said Mrs Henderson-Smythe. As she dragged her daughter away from the lens Nigel caught her mutter, '*All that money on school fees and just listen to her vocabulary.*'

The camera moved again.

'*Professor Livingstone, you were in the resort doing research. What thoughts will you be taking back to your university?*'

'*I will be writing a major piece about this experience from the multiple perspectives of all those participants in this liminal experiment in sustainable tourism development. It'll be published in a leading academic journal, early next year.*'

'I'm sure your peers will be riveted – not,' I thought.

'*I could summarise my approach…*'

'*Thanks Professor, but I think we're out of time.*'

Nigel didn't need any head nod to cut that interview.

'*Before we cross back to our studio in London,*' I said straight to camera, '*let's have a final comment from our band of heroes.*'

'*Brill time. Didn't take any rubbish from those locals,*' said Rick.

'*Cool, just cool. Can I say hi to me mum? Definitely going to take her advice and stick to hang gliding on the Costa del Sol next year.*' Tom waved.

'*Well my name's Sharon but all my friends call me Shazza. I had a fantastic time. I met the one. Rick here is the man of my dreams. I'd like to come back here for my honeymoon... maybe next year?'*

'Ambushed by love, were we?' I asked sweetly. *'What a romantic story – perhaps your Rick would like to add a few words. Oh no, he seems to have disappeared.*

'He's pissed off without me... the bastard.'

'Shaz, we're on the news!' said her friend.

'Well it's not news to me that all guys are bastards. I say shoot the lot of them,' Shazza said.

'Oh dear, Tracey isn't it?' I asked. *'Would you like to say something about it all?'*

'I'm not sure what really happened,' Tracey replied. *'I thought that Yousef was okay... treated us fine... not like the terrorist stuff in the papers. He said his group needed to make a point. Something about tourists not ruining their way of life. Everyone should benefit and all that. Spoke really posh like. I thought Yousef was s'posed to be able to say what he wanted to say. Like when he was going to talk to you news people. But then he just got shot when he opened his mouth. Why did the guys with the big guns do that?'*

'You'll have to ask the Ministry of Defence about that one. We don't make the headlines. I just report what's happening,' I said.

'And now, our final comments from the Henderson-Smythe's, whose daughter Tilly has been praised by everyone for her behaviour during what must have been a very scary holiday.'

'Unfortunate, we were just unfortunate to be caught up in a local squabble... unfortunate place, unfortunate time,' said Tilly's dad.

'Dreadful experience, after all we're British. I just want to say that I'm planning to sue the tour

operator and the hotel and the airline… ' said Tilly's mum, before her husband grabbed her arm and directed her towards the boarding gate.

'Tilly, you get the final word. Do you and that doll want to wave to all our viewers?'

Tilly faced Giselle, holding Jane aloft, and spoke clearly, *'Fuck off you slag.'*

47. Jane

Cyberspace is one amazing place. Ah am humbled by the response ma blog has had to the call for action and justice... UNFAIR... GET EVEN... SIGN UP! Tilly and me agreed that Yousef should be... needed to be heard... even if he was dead... so we got ourselves one big plan to go viral.

Ah had the idea.

Tilly had the tools.

It took a lot of time and effort. We didn't sleep till it was done and uploaded.

We started with our blog, headed **Jane needs to do it with you.** Ah told our site visitors about what happened at the Garden of Eden Hotel. Ah asked WANT TO DO IT WITH JANE DOLL? Seems a lot of people on the planet did. We're talking six figures and counting.

I rate it as Internet heaven in earthly paradise.

JANE DOLL: blog bits and bobs

Attitude
Think that you can, then you will
Think that you can't then you won't

Jane playing PARADISE LOST with YOU

Update on the campaign to tell it how it really was

WOW – Play about Paradise Smashed is going to be one big success.
Since the call to get involved Jane says:
Thanks to the 1500 responses. Truth is news.

The script is finished. The voices are on WAV. The images are nearly done.
D-day is exactly 120 days after Paradise morphed into Purgatory.

Don't forget to link to PLAY in PARADISE on YouTube on D-day. Ratings count!!!

Vive our new world order!

RIP… YOUSEF

Re: Jane playing PARADISE LOST with YOU
<<<By Viral Vive >>>

Great work Jane Doll. Our group is ready to support a cyberspace slam.

Re: Jane playing PARADISE LOST with YOU
<<<By Bad Apple >>>

Politicians do it with everyone! Communicators do it long distance! When are we going to get to play in paradise Jane Doll?

Re: Jane playing PARADISE LOST with YOU
<<<By Sisterhood >>>

If Genghis Khan… we can too

Jane Doll… go you, go you, go you!

Re: Jane playing PARADISE LOST with YOU

<<<By Watch your back >>>

Remember the big boys Jane. They will come after you. Stay brave, keep safe.

48. Tilly

Psycho said she wanted us to talk about a subject that Jane and me had raised at an earlier session – restorative justice.

'You mean the Mrs Watson's stuff with Jeremy?' I asked.

'We can start with that if you like,' Psycho replied. 'One of the benefits of the process can be understanding why people behave the way they do. What good do you think came out of your teacher inviting Jeremy and the people he bullies to talk about it as a group?'

'Not a lot. Mrs Watson has to do it that way 'cause it's what the school rules say. But I know that Jeremy is never going to change. He's just learnt how not to get caught. Like I told you, he's sneaky. He even boasts he knows where the CCTV cameras are in the streets round the school. So he can get you. Jane and me know he's not ever going to play fair. No matter what Mrs Watson does. Or how many times she does it.

'SWMBO is always quoting stuff from those books she reads on child development. Tough love, she calls it. And she's spot on. Jane and me absolutely know, one hundred percent, that the only way to stop Jeremy is to play tough.'

'Like blackmail over the photograph?' Psycho asked.

'Yes and bomb dives in the pool. He's a wuss in water.'

'Do you get angry that Jeremy can get away with being a bully?'

'Not angry, not now, 'cause I can sort Jeremy out. He's not that bright. Mrs Watson does what she can. She's not allowed to do the tough stuff. Jane says Mrs Watson operates under a handicap 'cause she can ONLY use that tool you call restorative justice – shame really. If she could use the BEST way to solve the problem, then there would be justice. And there'd be some hope for Jeremy.'

'What do you think Mrs Watson should be able to do to Jeremy?'

'Give him some of his own back. Bit like those people who get jabs done so they won't get a disease. You get a bit sick after they give it to you. But you don't die later. Mrs Watson should make Jeremy suffer and see how he likes it.'

'That sounds more like revenge.'

'If it works then it's good. Problem solved. The good guys win,' I argued. Jane dug me in the ribs. Right on, my friend, that dig meant.

'You want to tell me how you would provide justice, Tilly?' Psycho asked.

'For Jeremy, I would make everyone laugh at him. Like pull his swimmers off and push him in the deep end of the pool. He can't swim very well so he'd be scared. Then when he finally got to the edge and had to climb up the ladder, out of the water, we'd all see his willy. Or if he punched anyone or did anything mean, then I'd expose him – like on the social networking sites for kids, maybe even Facebook.

'For Giselle I'd invite her to come and do a story that I know she'd really, really want to put on television. Then when I'd got her waiting, I'd turn off the lights and lock her in the room for a whole hour with lots of spiders. I'd have a secret camera and record her freaking out. And then I'd unlock the room and give her a cup of camomile tea to calm her down. So she'd know I wasn't being cruel, just fair.'

'You think Giselle would thank you for a cup of tea?'

Jane and me nodded. I said to Psycho, 'Duh – definitely. SWMBO says there's nothing like a good cuppa to cement a friendship. Jane and me reckon my Mum hasn't got too many friends 'cause she drinks wine with most of the women that visit our house.

'I'd tell that Giselle if she didn't tell the whole truth ever

211

again, I'd upload the footage showing her with the spiders onto the Internet. When it went viral, she'd be a joke. Her career would be kaput.'

'Tilly, I'm going to have to disagree with you on those tactics. It may be a solution but I'm not convinced that they're positive ways forward. Have you thought about the risk? What if the Jeremys and Giselles in this world felt resentful of what you put on the Internet? That might make the situation worse? In my experience, angry people don't often do positive actions,' said Psycho.

'You agree with this restorative justice approach to crime and punishment?' I asked.

'I've seen that it can be successful in lots of conflict situations between people. The process is widely used now in schools and communities to help build understanding. Research confirms that this approach can reduce tension and stop fighting.'

'So what would you do to make it fair?' I wanted to know.

'Ah Tilly, I can't answer that one. I'm not angry with Jeremy or Giselle. I haven't suffered because of their actions. I don't need to hear their apologies.

'But I do believe that to solve something that's a big issue to you, you have to agree it's your problem and then find a solution that you can live with and other people can agree on. Then it stops being a problem. We psychologists call it closure.'

'What is the point of an apology when what Jeremy and Giselle did was deliberate? An apology is nothing if you're a meannie. It's just words. You can play lots of games with words.'

'Can you tell when someone apologises if they really mean it?' Psycho asked.

'Duh, of course,' I replied after looking at Jane who was

shaking her head in despair. Jane has been disillusioned with grown-ups since the holiday.

I explained to Psycho that, 'Some people, especially if you don't know them, are good at pretending. So you might think they were really sorry but they're just being good actors. Like those people who cry on TV who say their kids have disappeared. But really they've done murders. They cry but it's not 'cause they're sorry. They're trying to fool the police.'

'The important lesson about that is they don't fool the police, do they?' said Psycho. 'Those examples show people lying about, not apologising for, something done. I think the point I want to make is that we are good at working out whether someone is sincere about what they say. Young people are often better than adults.'

'Jane and me don't get how restor...ar...ra, this RJ thing, works if it's just talky games.'

'That's the point. RJ, as you call it, isn't a game. The term's a mouthful to say but restorative justice is a well-respected approach. Everybody harmed by the crime or the conflict, together with those who caused the damage, have to face each other and talk through what happened and why they did what they did. The result is that everyone has to agree their part and accept responsibility for their actions. The next steps work at how to repair the damage, physical and emotional, in order to find a positive way forward.'

I looked at Jane. She rolled her eyes. Jane and me thought it sounded dead boring – real rent speak.

Psycho kept talking. 'Let me give you an example. A young man sprayed paint over a car belonging to an elderly couple who lived nearby. When the two sides met, the young man said he did it because the old man told him off for throwing empty beer cans in their driveway and the old woman always turned her back when the young man walked past.

'He said that the old folks showed no respect and anyway they had got insurance. He couldn't see the problem.

'The old people told their side of the story. They spent their time and money on their garden. They said it was wrong that young people didn't respect all their hard work in the garden.

'The young man replied he didn't throw the beer cans into their garden. It must have been someone else.

'The old man said he couldn't tell one young person from another. They all wear hoodies and he couldn't see their faces.

'The old lady told how she had been pushed over by a young man in a hoodie when she was walking on the footpath.

'During the RJ session both sides were able to bring up what they felt were the issues. Can you see what they might have learnt from the discussion, Tilly?'

'Well the young man did what he did to the car 'cause the old man told him off for something he didn't do like throwing the beer cans. And the old lady was rude to the young man 'cause he wore a hoodie and she's scared when she sees young men dressed like that.'

'Exactly,' Psycho agreed, 'all that anger didn't generate any positive solutions. But when they faced each other and talked about it, both parties realised how the other side felt.'

'So what happened after they all finished talking?'

'The young man apologised for his vandalism. He cleaned the paint off the car. The old man apologised for shouting things that were not true. The old lady said she would always be scared of hoodies. However she promised that she would try to remember that all young people were not the same. I understand that she says hello and waves now whenever she sees that young man and his friends. Better way to live life, Tilly?'

214

'In that case, maybe. I bet that old lady will never trust a hoodie though. Just like me and Jane are never going to believe that Jeremy is going to turn into a good guy. And what about Yousef? He didn't get a chance to sit and talk with anyone. Even though Giselle promised him he would.'

'I agree with you Tilly, that restorative justice isn't the only way to solve conflict. But it's worth considering.'

'Jane and me are going to think on how you link RJ with Machiavelli and Tuckman,' I told her. Jane smirked. Like she believed that was going to happen any time soon.

'I will look forward to hearing your views on that,' Psycho said. 'I'm sure it'll be very original. I can honestly say that I've never read anything that links those three approaches.

But I do know that living with anger inside you is not healthy. That anger builds and builds until it shows on the outside. Some people get headaches, others get pains in their guts. And some people don't sleep.'

'Oh are we going back to the sleep thingy? I already told you. I can sleep. I will sleep. It's a short term thing. I have to look after Jane until she finishes our project. It's something we need to do. After all, I made Yousef a promise. And it's wrong to break your promise.'

'Are you going to explain that promise to me?'

Tilly shook her head and pulled Jane closer.

'What sort of project are you doing with Jane?' Psycho asked.

'It's a secret at the moment,' I explained. Jane was not happy about this conversation I could tell. Her lips were pursed.

'I thought it was safe to share secrets about this holiday when we were all in this room.'

'Not this one. I want it to be a complete surprise.'

'That makes me feel nervous, Tilly. Something that's

215

so secret you have to stop sleeping to do it. Something that you can't share with people who really care about you, like your parents, Mrs Watson or even me,' Psycho said quietly.

'Oh don't worry,' I told her. 'It's nothing scary. Like I'm not making a bomb over the Internet to get Giselle or anything.

'I could you know, make a bomb. Jane found six sites that tell you what you need. We could make one in the bathroom. Dead simple if you know a bit of chemistry. But you'll think it's cool, what Jane is doing. It may even be a type of RJ. A positive way forward for the world to hear everyone's version. Jane says, it's a watch this space, suck it and see, trick and treat kind of verdict on the truth!'

Psycho looked anxious. Maybe she wasn't going to sleep either.

49. Jane

JANE DOLL: blog bits and bobs

Attitude
Think that you can, then you will
Think that you can't then you won't

Premiere with Jane in PARADISE LOST

D-day for our sensational new play. The truth will be out there from November 30.

The link is You Tube

Hit it and help spread the revolution.

THANK YOU

Re: Premiere with Jane in PARADISE LOST
<<<By Tilly>>>

Jane Doll, U R a star!. Hollywood bite your butt!!!

Re: Premiere with Jane in PARADISE LOST
<<<By Bad Apple >>>

You seen my bite, Jane Doll. When do I see yours? Nibble, nibble, up your bum.

50. Tilly

It was my last session with Psycho. Jane and me were going to miss her in a weird sort of way. I quite liked sitting in her office, talking about stuff and eating chocolates. Jane said it was time to get out. Deep and meaningful was dangerous.

Psycho had a report sitting on the table when we arrived. It had my name on it.

'Are you going to let me and Jane read your report?' I asked when we had made ourselves comfortable on the usual chair opposite her.

'No, it's confidential,' Psycho said.

'It's about me isn't it? So why can't I read it?'

'You didn't commission or pay for the report, Tilly. Therefore, it does not belong to you. It's about you but not yours.'

'Can I buy a copy?'

'Legally, you're a minor. So no, you can't have access, paid or not.'

'Sucks, so unfair.'

'It might seem that way but it's all in your own interest. I'm happy to tell you what I think though. If you want.'

'You going to say I'm bonkers?'

'No Tilly, I'm not. That word is not in my professional vocabulary. We discussed that at our first meeting, remember?'

I sighed and looked at Jane.

'What's the matter, Tilly?'

'SAMO, SAMO,' I said. When Psycho looked confused I reminded her about Basquiet and his street art. She nodded.

'I regard you as one of my all-time favourite clients, Tilly. I'm going to frame your drawings and put them up on the wall in that corner near the window. The one you did of

218

me I'm going to hang above my desk. What do you think about that?'

I just shrugged. 'Not my drawings, Jane did them. It's just bits of paper and coloured pens. Any kid could do them.'

'She probably says that to all her patients,' Jane whispered. 'Grown-ups, what did you expect, Tilly, a medal for the golden paintbrush award?'

'I will really, really miss our chats. Poke my eye and hope to die,' smiled Psycho. She didn't seem too keen on my silence and conversation with Jane.

'Can Jane and me have a chocolate?' I asked.

'No. Too much sugar isn't good for you,' Psycho replied.

'How come you let me eat chocolates before?'

'Those other sessions were really tough. It's good to have a treat sometimes. Today is not a tough session. No chocolates but I've got some roasted pumpkin seeds if you're interested?'

'Oh no, not health food.'

'I'll take that as a no. Want me to start with my conclusions and recommendations?'

'Sounds like parents' evening at school. Is it going to be boring?'

'Boring is one word that nobody would ever use to describe you, Matilda Henderson-Smythe. You're clever, funny and talented. I can honestly say I have never had the pleasure of meeting a champion chess player who sings, swims and wins photographic competitions. You are in a very special league of teenagers. How am I doing on the boring school evenings' scale?'

'Cool – you put those things in the report?'

'Yes and more.'

'This is where you say BUT, isn't it?'

219

'Do you want to explain to me what you mean by that?'

'Well teachers always say something good about you. Then they say BUT. Then you get to hear all the stuff they don't like about you. SWMBO makes notes at that stage. We have to have a family debrief when we get home. I'm not allowed chocolates then either.'

'Tilly, I don't think you have Post Traumatic Stress Disorder, in its conventional presentation. You are a remarkable and very insightful young lady. I can feel your anger at the unfairness of what happened to Yousef. He didn't get a fair chance to say what he needed to. Adult games are played by adult rules. People thought he had a real gun with real bullets. Sometimes bad things happen to well-intentioned plans.

'I do think there is a link between what happened on your holiday and why you don't sleep.'

'You are right. There is or there used to be. Two nights ago me and Jane slept right through. I haven't yawned once in class since then.'

'Well done. Do you feel these sessions helped?'

'Is this kind of constructive feedback stuff? Like Tuckman's survey. You want me to rank you on the forming, norming, storming or performing scale? Do I get a prize?'

'Tilly, you're quite a delight. You can give feedback however you want. No prizes, nothing's right or wrong. It can be according to Tuckman, Machiavelli or the man in the moon.'

'Oh, you mean the informal anecdotal stuff, like they talk about on the Internet... not really my scene. Coming here has been okay. Better than writing essays that's for sure. I think you should have a big sofa though... like the shrinks on television. They have bottles of Vodka in their desk drawers... medicinal... for the debrief. That usually means having a shag with the older doctor after the client leaves crying.'

'I can see I'll have to watch some of these shows to see what my competition is offering.'

'Your chocolates are a big winner. They don't have them on the TV.'

'Let's keep my advantage a secret between us, shall we?'

'Does that mean Jane and me can have one?'

'No, it's pumpkin seeds or nothing. Shall I tell you what I've recommended for managing your next steps?'

'You sound like my grandmother,' I told her.

'The one you told me about, Edwina Thaddeus Henderson -Smythe? Wasn't she the one with the cat called Freya that had a problem with trapped wind?'

'That's her. You want to hear what Jane told me about a conversation she heard between SWMBO and Granny?'

Psycho nodded.

'Shall I tell you how I manage Tilly?' SWMBO said.

'Managing Tilly?' laughed my Granny. 'Is that an oxymoron or wishful thinking?'

'I didn't really get the joke but Jane said my grandmother was a regular hoot.'

'I found Jane's drawings very interesting,' said Psycho. 'They helped me understand how you both saw some of the people you told me about. I know I had your photographs. They made sure I could remember who was who. But Jane's drawings gave me a way of seeing how others might see these people. Would you like them back? They belong to Jane but I'm guessing she'd be happy for you to look after them.'

I whispered to Jane before replying, 'No, Jane says it's her present to you. She wants to know if you're really going to put them in a frame, like you said before.'

'Of course I am, Tilly. I wouldn't lie to you. Like we agreed poke my eye and hope to die.'

I looked at Jane. She blinked. It was okey dokey.

'You could tell everyone that Jane is the one that survived. The enemy didn't get her.'

'That's a thought Tilly, very kind of Jane. Can I thank her direct?'

I looked at Jane again. She scowled.

'Okay, but don't touch her,' I said to Psycho. 'You can just salute.'

Psycho responded as requested. Jane smiled at me although Psycho couldn't see her. It seemed like a sense of occasion.

'I'll give you permission to use my photographs as well,' I added, 'then when I'm famous you can sell them and get rich.'

'I shall consider that an honour, Tilly. Perhaps you will buy a Jackson Pollock to hang on your wall. And I will have a Matilda Henderson-Smythe on mine.'

'AND a Jane Doll,' I reminded her.

'And a Jane Doll,' agreed Psycho. 'There is something else I would like to talk about. Tilly; I do have concerns about how you deal with anger. Seeking revenge doesn't have a good track record.'

'It gets results doesn't it?'

'Perhaps but not in a way that makes you feel at peace. For example how are you going to stop being angry with Giselle? She didn't mean for Yousef to get shot. She didn't know his gun was a toy gun. Neither did the soldiers. Or all the people he kept as hostages. Even you and Jane thought he had a real gun until the end. It's a mess but not your mess. Your life is for you to live your way.'

'No problems. I've worked it out.'

'Want to share that path with me?'

'Jane and me found out about this man called Gandhi. He got shot too. I asked my teacher, Mrs Watson, about him. She told me that one of the most famous things he said was that you have to be the change you wish to see in the world. So after talking to you, Jane and me decided to take responsibility.'

'How did you do that?'

'It's easier if I show you what we did. You want to see? It's on YouTube.'

'What's on YouTube?'

'The truth.'

'I'm not following, Tilly.'

'Jane and me brought you our present. It's a play we wrote. We called it Jane Doll's Paradise Lost. You're going to love it.'

'Am I?'

'It's right out there, restorative justice for the world. Jane and me think it's only fair that we name you as one of the people that helped make it happen.'

'I'm starting to feel a bit nervous Tilly. What have you done?'

'Oh you don't have to be scared. You'll probably get thousands of requests from people who want to pay you to listen to them.'

'That isn't making me feel any better.'

Psycho definitely looked a bit tense.

'Look and learn. It all boils down to attitude. Think that you can, then you will. That's what Jane used to say on her blog.'

'Your doll has a blog site?'

'Yes, we started one before we went on holidays to the Garden of Eden Hotel. You wouldn't believe some of the crazy messages we got.'

'I probably would but let's skip that for now. How come you didn't mention this during our interview sessions?'

'You didn't ask. I can give you the details if you want to follow. There are some seriously disturbed men out there who really, really need your help. Try reading Bad Apple. He's creepy and sex starved.'

'Tilly, I'm concerned about this. Do you parents know what you've been doing on the Internet?'

'No way, SWMBO would go spare. You promised anything I said in here stayed in here.'

'It does. But you might be involved in activities that adults consider unsafe, maybe even illegal.'

'Not any longer. Now we've got justice for Yousef and gutted that Giselle, me and Jane are giving up the blog. We're going to win the school chess championship for special needs pupils next year So I need to spend all my time on chess.'

'That sounds like a healthy goal. But please finish telling me about this play. Paradise Lost? That's quite a famous title.'

'We know. That way lots of people will come across it when they're doing research on that boring, old poem. Jane and me didn't really get it the whole Milton thing. But it's very popular. So Milton is kind of helping us with distribution – process of association and all that.'

Psycho didn't look all that happy with this news.

'Jane got lots of people on her blog to help her,' I told Psycho, 'so that Yousef could give his message to the world. She used her drawings to show some of the characters. You'll see that the Tour Operator in the play has a face just like her drawing of Wayne. The one that you can put on your wall.'

Psycho nodded and asked, 'How will this help Yousef?'

'Our play means that Giselle doesn't get the last word.

Our play's gone viral. Giselle's a goner. If you connect you get to watch our very first production. And here's all our words written down.'

With that Jane and me handed a copy of our script. It was titled:

PARADISE LOST
by
DOLL FACE.

A one act play for the Internet dedicated to Yousef who was shot for trying to tell the truth... even though he didn't have a real gun.

This play is performed by puppets to protect the identity of the main characters.
But we know who you are!
And you know who you are too!!!

Psycho was speechless.

Jane winked and blinked twice. That means we don't tell Psycho we plan to set up a WhatsApp group to keep in contact with all our fans. Giselle will never be able to catch us! Jane says I've got to make a final decision and exclude Rude Boy, Bad Apple, from the group.

I know Jane's right but where's the fun? I tell Jane to watch this space!

~~~~~~~~

Mosaic Down Syndrome

- Down syndrome is a condition in which a person has an extra chromosome. One in every 1,000 babies is born with Down's. Distinctive physical characteristics, developmental challenges, medical conditions and learning difficulties are often associated with the syndrome.

- There are three types of Down syndrome, of which Mosaic Down syndrome is rare. Approximately 1 in 27,000 people are diagnosed with Mosaic Down syndrome.

- Mosaic Down syndrome affects about 2% of the people with Down syndrome. Mosaic means mixture or combination. For children with Mosaic Down syndrome, some of their cells have 3 copies of chromosome 21, but other cells have the typical two copies of chromosome 21. Children with mosaic Down syndrome may have the same features as other children with Down syndrome. However, they may have fewer features of the condition due to the presence of some (or many) cells with a typical number of chromosomes.

- One American study of 30 children and one Japanese study of 8 children compared them with matched children having standard Down syndrome, and their findings suggest that groups of children with Mosaic Down syndrome have a higher average IQ.

- Some of the children with Mosaic Down syndrome do not actually look as if they have Down syndrome – the usual physical features are not obvious.

- This raises important social and identity issues for both parents and children,

- The majority of children with any form of Down syndrome require special therapy to assist with any developmental delays in speech and motor skills.

- Although mathematics can be challenging many Mosaic Down syndrome children excel in reading, writing and art.

For more information, see:

www.downs-syndrome.org.uk

www.nhs.uk/conditions/downs-syndrome

www.globaldownsyndrome.org

www.mosaicdownsyndrome.com

www.imdsa.org

www.ds-health.com/mosaic.htm

About the Author

Dianne Stadhams is an Australian, resident in the UK, who has worked globally in marketing and project management. With a PhD in visual anthropology she spent many years using creative tools – drama, dance, radio, video – to empower people in some of the world's poorest nations to communicate their vision of sustainable development. She believes passionately that the arts are valuable tools to promote social cohesion, provoke debate and influence attitudes and mind sets.

Her first book of short stories, *Links*, was published in 2019. Other short stories were published in the following anthologies (*Crackers* 2018, *Glit-e-rary* 2017, *Baubles* 2016, *Snowflakes* 2015, *Recognition* 2009). Two novels were shortlisted in the Triskele Global Competitions (*Doll Face* 2018, *Crocodile Tears* 2016); two plays selected by Bristol Old Vic for workshop development (*Never Black or White* 2017, *Aftermath* 2016); *Sh*t* was selected for a workshop production at the Croydon Warehouse in 2004.

Screen scripts include *Tada the Dancing Drum* (television series to promote literacy in Africa 2010): *Pascale's People* (Dulwich Festival London, Creteil International Festival of Women in Film, France 2005):

Tourism in The Gambia, a television documentary made with and for Gambia Television (screened at Royal Anthropological Institute's International Film Festival, Le Festival du Quartier Film Festival Senegal 2003, Italian Ethnographic International Film Festival 2004): *Beyond the Brochure* (Toura D'Ora International Film Festival, Germany 2001).

For further information and to follow Dianne:

www.stadhams.com

www.facebook.com/dianne.stadhams.1

www.amazon.co.uk/Links-What-happens-Dianne-Stadhams/dp/1907335633

www.bridgehousepublishing.co.uk/index.php/buy-our-books

Other Publications by Bridge House Imprints

Links

by Dianne Stadhams

LINKS – sometimes random, many times unplanned, often with far reaching consequences, always shaping our journey from cradle to grave – the stuff of life.

Just how do Atta Gatta the child-eating crocodile, Scheherazade the pantomime star and Judy the stammering Goth strategically connect characters across the globe?

Enjoy this trilogy of inter-linked short stories that will make you smile and squirm as they raise questions about the needs and challenges of our contemporary world.

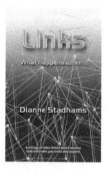

Order from Amazon:

Paperback: ISBN 978-1-907335-63-1
eBook: ISBN 978-1-907335-64-8

Spooking

by Gill James

Tom crashes his car and he wakes up in an unfamiliar place. He
is unable to reach Amanda. They argued just before the crash.
He meets cheeky but friendly Marcus, who, though younger
than Tom, has more experience in the areas that now matter. But
Marcus has his own concerns and eventually has to leave Tom
to deal with his problems on his own. How can Tom let Amanda
know how much he loves her? Does she feel the same way? Will
they ever be able to move forward?

Order from Amazon:

Paperback: ISBN 978-1-907335-42-6
eBook: ISBN 978-1-907335-43-3

XY

by Shanta Everington

Fifteen-year-old Jesse lives in a society where babies are born neither male nor female – gender is assigned at birth. Will the secret she closely guards be found out? Boyfriend Zeus, mother Ana's Natural Souls, and new friend Ork, leader of We Are One, pull Jesse in different directions, forcing her to make her own mind up about who she really is.

"A highly original and thought-provoking dystopian novel. I don't think I've ever read anything like it!"
(Luisa Plaja, Chicklish, the UK's Teen Fiction Site)

Order from Amazon:

Paperback: ISBN 978-1-907335-32-7
eBook: ISBN 978-1-907335-34-1

CPSIA information can be obtained
at www.ICGtesting.com
Printed in the USA
LVHW012138210221
679514LV00004B/301